PRAISE FOR REPLACEMENT PARTS

"There are no holds barred in Marc Dickinson's rich and fearless collection of stories. He dives deep in America's dark soul—the addictions, the detentions, the diseases, the layoffs, the divided communities—and returns to the surface with pure gold. The closer Dickinson brings us to tragedy, the more he attunes us to the beauty and kindness that might save us all. You will come away from this book wiser, more compassionate, and more hopeful."

-Bonnie Jo Campbell, author of *American Salvage* and *Mothers, Tell Your Daughters*

"These stories by Marc Dickinson present us with characters who have led tough, hardscrabble lives. He writes beautifully about both lucky and unlucky people, and this book has the great virtues of compassion and keen observation."

-Charles Baxter, author of *The Sun Collective* and *Feast of Love*

"The ordinary lives chronicled in *Replacement Parts* are chronicled with extraordinary grace. These characters are often lonely and soul-sick, struggling to make ends meet, but we're very glad to be in their company, because Marc Dickinson explores their lives with heart and intelligence, helping us better understand the beautiful, redemptive struggle of the human condition."

-Benjamin Percy, author of *The Ninth Metal*, *Red Moon*, and *Thrill Me*

"In these loving, devastating stories, generations of parents and children, lovers and friends and neighbors, struggle to do right by each other in small towns and harsh landscapes that don't make it easy. How do people make a future, or even envision one, in circumstances that feel both unchangeable and precarious? Marc Dickinson has written a vivid, poignant, powerful book about people and communities trying to find a way forward."

-Caitlin Horrocks, author of *Life Among the Terranauts* and *The Vexations*

STORIES

MARC DICKINSON

REPLACEMENT PARTS

atmosphere press

For Laurie, Chloe, and Eli

The Midwest is like a ghost in my life.

—Tim O'Brien

We whizzed along down through the skeleton
remnants of Iowa...Glaciers had crushed this
region in the time before history. There'd been
a drought for years...All the false visions had
been erased. It felt like the moment before the
Savior comes. And the Savior did come, but we
had to wait a long time.

—Denis Johnson, *Jesus' Son*

TABLE OF CONTENTS

FOOD. GAS. VACANCY.

Drake lived in our shed for a month during the summer. At least that's what we called it. The shed, our shack, a hut held up by the air itself. Not that it matters much out here where every shape seems made from sun and dust. Sometimes, it seems Dexton, Iowa, isn't just where two counties cross paths, but where one drought turns into another, doubling up the heat.

In other words, it's nowhere for a pretty girl to be raised, which is why for class photos, Mom dressed me in clothes that covered each inch of skin—overalls and work boots—making it impossible to tell me apart from other short-haired school-boys. A late bloomer in every way.

But this year, when sixteen rolled around, there was no hiding anymore. With the gangly legs and undeniable chest, I became a reluctant member of the girl race, forever and ever, amen.

So no wonder, before she died, I'd often catch Mom gazing at me with eyes slit, as if blaming my body—healthy and spreading—for the cancer eating her from the inside out.

***

3

Our trailer sat on the edge of town, which once upon a time was a solitary way station on a road to nowhere. Then Highway 20 came along and forced us to become just another name on the map. At least that's what Mom said. But this was before I was born, because all I've ever known is a place separated by a quiet two-lane: one side with a convenience store parked next to a pile of double-wides, while across the street sat an empty motel with a bar feeding off lost travelers.

Still, regardless of the reports every few years about missing girls, women foolish enough to follow strangers into the fields, somehow men still wound up in our trailer. And no doubt my mother was beautiful back then. Nothing but curves and cleavage, all that hair hanging down.

So last year, when the guys began to look me up and down instead, Mom would offer the car keys and tell me to disappear. But no matter how long I stayed away, I'd end up walking in on something. Each night I had to sneak to my room, as if nobody knew I was even there, while various boys made their noises down the hall, only to leave the next morning like a quick mist.

Except now that's actually what I like to remember most, days when her body moved like water, instead of those last months when her blouses suddenly sat flat against her chest. Her skin smelling like the vitamin E she rubbed on her scars. How none of it mattered when a few weeks later everything settled into her bones. And with both of us so far away from any kind of help, sometimes it's hard not to blame Dexton for her fate. Like the land itself had run out of options.

But during those last few weeks, when boyfriends stopped by, Mom still made me trace her lips in red, slather on the bright blue eyeshadow. I pulled her arms into leopard-print blouses. Slipped on flame-red pants that were once skin-tight and now hung loose on her hips. Then she'd send me away again. In fact, it was only when Dad arrived back on the scene that she demanded I stick around, treat him nice, as if we were finally a family once more.

***

When Dad rolled up on a cloud of fumes, I figured he was just another lover paying his respects. But then I saw his freshly shaved face and knew he was different. He looked like a rock star, a cowboy, something from TV. Nothing like the other men who showed up. This guy walked at a faster clip. Didn't smell of 30-weight oil. And seemed sober when he strolled through our gate.

"Nothing changes here, does it?" he said, studying the trailer end to end. "Still standing."

I led him inside and pointed to her room. He smiled and said I was just as lovely as ever.

Mom mostly slept, fatigue arriving so fast you'd be talking to yourself before seeing she dozed off. So it wasn't long until he was out on the porch again, asking me if I recalled his face.

I shook my head. "She's only got a little time left. I'd save the lines for her."

"Lovely but tough, huh?" His shaggy blond hair fluttered like a ribbon in the wind.

"Maybe. Maybe not." I dug at the grit under my toenails. The streetlights were turning on as all the neon signs around town slowly came into focus: *Food. Gas. Vacancy.*

"Yeah, you look tough enough." His leathers creaked like a worn-out chair as he sat down and put an arm around my shoulders. But unlike most of the men who visited, his hands didn't start to wander when he said, "Just like your mama."

The day Drake first arrived at our trailer court, despite the dreads hanging like a bead curtain down his back, I quickly saw a sharp echo of myself. With a face full of lonesome, he looked somehow misplaced, just lingering around the lane. One moment, up against a light pole. The next, gone entirely. At first, he watched from afar, as if I was a model showing how things work. This is how we eat cereal on the porch. This is when you're supposed to go to bed and how to avoid it. This is what we wear while working at the gas station: *Hello, My Name is Hannah.*

Then one morning, he simply appeared on our stoop, the sun already electric.

"What's your name?" I asked, sneaking up behind him as if he were a feral stray.

He didn't flinch, didn't even turn around. "If you want me to leave, ask nice."

"Did I say that?"

His black braids were little anchors holding his head in place. When he stood, I saw a face not much older than mine. And when he held out a hand, I put mine inside his, our clasp hanging between us like an unanswered prayer. We were two bronze statues, my skin tanned from living in this endless oven of a summer. But his was different. Almost close to chocolate but sunnier than that, as if a light radiated from within his body, turning his dark skin bright.

He looked me up and down with his ice-chip eyes. "You're beautiful."

"You're weird," I said, pulling back my hand. "Don't you have somewhere else to be?"

"I don't know," he said. "Seems like a good place to be."

"You kidding?" I squinted back, a common kind of expression around here. "It's almost 100 degrees. And it's not through yet."

"It's perfect." His crooked teeth tumbled through the smile. They looked like a bunch of rocks falling in front of one another. "Don't you think?"

I didn't though. I had absolutely no idea what to think.

After the funeral, Dad stuck around. It was Mom's last request, outside of spreading her ashes in a nearby field. And though the man was practically a stranger, it didn't seem all that strange. In fact, it was a comfort of sorts. There were actual tears when he threw Mom to the wind, as if that pasture meant something secret. Plus, his face was never hungry. He kept his eyes to himself. At times, he even looked so soft and sweet it was close to having a real-life pet.

But as soon as she was scattered, Dad didn't waste time getting rid of the clutter.

"Past is nothing but a roadblock," he said, tossing Mom's skirts in the garbage.

"Maybe I wanted those," I said, knowing that wasn't true.

"People offer good money for these things." I wasn't sure which people he was referring to, but it was nice to have an adult around for once, taking care any way he saw fit. He put on gloves before touching her sheets. The empty vials of morphine. Those half-filled glasses of water that never fully put out the fire in her throat. I told him cancer wasn't contagious, but he kept right on holding his breath until the trash bag was out of sight on the other side of our fence.

That night he left, and I just assumed he was gone for good—another part-time parent.

Then two days later, he walked back into the trailer and opened a beer. I didn't ask where he'd been, knowing silence was sometimes the best way to keep speaking to one another. But he must've seen the question in my face when he winked and said, "Trying to find you a new mom."

"They were never in large supply around here."

Dad patted my hand and offered me a drink from his bottle. But I waved it away because he obviously didn't get it. One mother had been enough. Another just felt like replacement parts.

When the heat index got dangerous, Dad took another trash bag down to the pawn shop and came back with a plastic pool.

7

Muggy days, when the sweat became too much, we'd sit in it and spray ourselves with a withered garden hose. I wore one of Mom's old bikinis. Dad dipped his feet in the water, catnapping. And Drake stayed across the street, until one day we saw him drag a couch down our lane, cutting a small path in the gravel. He couldn't get the sofa through our gate, struggled to lift it over the chain-link. Eventually, he left it in the road and sat on our porch, wearing those dirty khakis, his hiking boots just about torn in two.

Dad sprayed his knees and said, "If you want a day job, stealing isn't it."

"I didn't steal it." Drake bit his lip and grinned. "It was just lying there."

Dad nodded. "You definitely got a mind for it."

The couch had sat out so long nobody would even know it was missing. One thing we weren't short on was spare furniture acting as lawn ornaments. But nobody paid much mind out here, our road never more than a pit stop, a quick blur from one place to the next. So I helped him lift the couch onto the porch. None of the springs were broken. Perfect for sunset-sitting.

That night, Drake and I watched the purple overcome the sky when he asked about Mom.

"She's not around anymore."

"Mine either," he said. "Dad went back to Mexico to get her. But that was a month ago."

"That was about the time my mom took off."

"You're lucky to still have *him* around."

I wasn't so sure. Dad sealed a leak in the roof, though it hadn't rained in weeks. He raked our gravel. Even attached a basketball hoop to the old telephone pole at our dead end—for all the trailer kids to share. But mostly it just sat, idle as a lightning rod: more dead wood nobody needed hanging around. "He's pretty new to all this. We're more roommates than anything."

8

"I'd take a roommate." Drake's voice was all but begging to stay, even if just for a bit.

But I wouldn't ask that of him. I liked him too much already. He'd be better off moving to someplace where waiting around wasn't your only option.

Drake didn't show for a few days, at last catching my drift. Still, for a place where goodbye was a way of life, I couldn't shake the sadness: another misbegotten boy, put upon and left behind.

Until we saw him dragging a rug down the lane, and I knew he wasn't going anywhere.

Dad was impressed. "Resourceful little thing, isn't he?"

I splashed water on my legs, sprouting bleach-blonde hair that was almost invisible except to the touch.

Dad helped pull the rug over the fence. It smelled bad and looked stained. And that's when he offered the shed. "Nothing much but a roof to keep out of the sun."

Drake scratched his elbow, dry and ashy. "My parents will be looking for me."

"Sure, sure. Just in the meantime. With a gift like yours, it's best to stay under cover."

Drake said he didn't pickpocket, didn't shoplift. He was a good kid, he kept telling us.

"You *are* a good kid," Dad said, standing close behind me. "With brown skin."

Drake looked at the couch he'd offered in exchange for some company. And now here he was being handed a new home, even if it was out back in a shack. "What's the catch?"

Dad laid his hands on my shoulders. His fingers were freezing, as if somehow untouched by the heat. "What you think, Hannah? Isn't it about time you had a brother around here?"

I didn't say yes or no. I couldn't even shrug under his

weight. I just gazed at Drake, my dark-skinned twin, and knew our little family had just gotten one boy bigger.

Mom never talked about Dad. All my life I heard how a man gone missing wasn't worth the time it took to speak his name. But his absence was larger than any one body could fill. It was probably why there were so many other men around with their gleaming trucks and rusty beards, watery tattoos smearing their arms. At the gas station, I'd see them come and go, each the same as the rest: hard-shelled and licking their chops as I moved from one pump to the next. And this was probably why I was still a virgin. Whenever I took a man's money and his winks, they all had bottomless eyes that'd break a heart real easy if you let them. But Mom could never resist.

Only thirty-three when she passed, my mother always appeared so much older. It's what this place does to women. I've seen photos in her old yearbook, looking more like myself than I care to admit. But when I was twelve and felt my first cramp, saw all that red coming out of me, it was the school nurse who said I wasn't dying, who told me this is what it meant to be a woman. *Part of our burden and blessing.* And when I told Mom, she just rolled her eyes and said she didn't need rivals stealing her show. Of course, she tried to smile, as if it was just for laughs—until each eye started to follow me around the room instead, and I knew it was no joke.

But, despite the wear and tear, Mom could still have anyone worth wanting. She wasn't just a mother to me but to every man who set sight on her. I had all the big brothers I could handle, each gone by the break of the sun, heading off into the barren fields where all the rest of the bodies were buried. Until, of course, the cancer took hold of her like a permanent passerby.

Except now that she's gone, I often get a fierce little feeling she's still around. Not nearby, but out wandering the wilderness. Other times, it's as if she'd never really been here at all, like some kind of mirage only half-dying men could see from afar—then up-close quickly vanished.

At hand, she was nowhere to be found, but from a distance looked good enough to drink.

The first day of July, the thermometer ready to pop, another film crew rolled through. They always chose the worst time of year, our town teeming with heat waves and warnings.

At the station, as they filled their tanks, Drake slipped behind the counter as if leery of strangers. Most days he stayed with Dad, trading tales about the road, though none of the stories added up to much or gave any hint of where they'd been. By the time I got home, they'd be off to bed, tired from talking themselves in circles. But today Drake tagged along, looking pale and full of the fidgets. I figured the humidity was finally getting to him.

A guy wearing a Hawaiian shirt handed over a credit card. I gave it a swipe, and as the machine tallied the numbers and sent them to the satellites, I studied those vans sitting outside.

Hollywood wasn't an uncommon thing to see. Iowa gave tax relief for them to come and make movies, add to tourism. So a few times a year they'd arrive and leave a tip or two before moving on. But there were never any real celebrities in tow to make a difference—at least none I recognized from the magazine covers spread around the store. "Anybody famous this time?"

"It isn't that kind of movie," said Hawaiian Shirt.

Drake sat up. "What kind of movie is it?"

"The no-budget kind." The guy took his card back, a smile plastered across his face. "Something about farmers growing pot, a Mexican cartel, a drug deal gone bad."

"You guys have some funny ideas about places," Drake said.

"The script also says we're supposed to be in Pennsylvania." Mr. Hollywood shrugged and signed the receipt with a squiggle. "What you going to do?"

I took the carbon copy from his hand. "I prefer comedies."

"Me too," he said, winking that same old wink. "With happy endings."

My skin heated up, his stare making me sweat. And though I should've told the guy to go to hell—had seen my mother do it countless times to boys who gave her the once-over—it was as if the words were hiding in my mouth. Like I was outside my body, watching this stupid girl let a man steal her voice with a single look. Instead, it was Drake who jumped to his feet, knocking over the stool with a newfound anger that was hard not to be flattered by.

"I think it's time for you to leave," he said.

The man offered a little laugh. "All right, kid. All right."

When he was gone, Drake said, "They don't know a thing about deals gone bad."

"Who cares about what they do or don't know?"

"What right do they have?" Drake glared at me and I felt ashamed, though of what I wasn't sure. "Coming here to tell us how we live."

"But it's not here that they're telling about, now is it?"

I laced my fingers into his, a small attempt at *thank you*, until he yanked his hand away as if shocked by some unforeseen spark.

"Do you go to school?" I asked one afternoon. In the distance, the sky was dark-clouded and full of menace, threatening to pour down a rain that never seemed to come.

"It's just a bunch of facts. Nothing anyone needs," he said, still panting from the game.

Dad and Drake spent mornings playing basketball, a one-on-one matchup that began innocently enough but soon verged on violence. They never kept score. And never called fouls, each guarding the other so close it was hard to tell one sweat-soaked body from the other. Drake was the first to tap out, calling it quits after Dad nearly wrestled the poor kid to the ground. Even now the boy's muscles still trembled, always unnerved by Dad's unexpected strength.

"A diploma gets you away quicker. That's what Mom said."

I almost smiled, but it didn't feel right on my mouth.

"She sounds smart," he said, wiping at his brow.

Drake suffered under that bulk of hair, as if he didn't know any better. The dreads were a fur pelt that needed a good shave. There's a reason every living thing with hair hides from the sun during the day—in this heat, we've all overcome the need to be human. But Drake seemed to lack the ability to adapt, and it'd get him in trouble someday. It's what I liked best about him.

"Well, my mom was full of all kinds of advice she didn't follow." The sun baked my skin a deep cherry, cooking me pink all the way through. So I slid into the empty pool, spraying my feet with the hose. "What's your mom like?"

Drake calmly looked at the horizon as if an answer was out there amongst the dead lawns and dirt. He wore one of Dad's Harley shirts, but his boots still looked liable to crumble, just asking to be put out of their misery. Soon the breeze started to whip the dry soil around.

"We should go in," I said. "There's a tornado watch tonight."

He tightly gripped the chair, like a branch set to snap. Like something that could detonate at the sound of a say-so. I wrapped up in a towel and stood behind him, stroking the strings of his hair. They didn't seem connected to anything actual, just a bunch of floating snakes in my hand. I wondered how long it'd take for someone like me to make hair like that.

"Ever think about doing something with this?"

He shook his head, the fat ropes on his head barely slithering.

"Wouldn't a trim feel better?"

"Then nobody would recognize me."

"I would." I made my fingers into a pair of scissors, laid a braid between them to feign a cut, when Drake grabbed my wrist. Who knew he could feel a thing through that network of hairy roots? And I was almost sorry until he let go, leaving behind a bruise. As he stormed inside, I wondered who this guy thought he was. Or who I wished him to be. But before I could figure it, a wind rose up and capsized our pool, as if I'd been the only thing holding it down all along.

By late July, Drake and Dad slept most of the day. At night, after a shift at the station, I'd come home to them on the couch, heads together as if getting ready to sell something to some-body.

When I opened the door, they'd break apart and tip their beer cans a bit too casually.

"How was work?" Dad asked, scratching his three-day stubble. He stank like a fish tank.

"Six hours and two customers."

"Pathetic," he said. "I can't believe this whole place doesn't just close down. I bet you didn't even earn enough to cover the station's light bill today."

"Earned enough to pay *ours*." I rubbed my feet, though most nights I sat on a stool studying for my dual-credit classes at Northern Community College. I planned to graduate early from Roosevelt High, then apply to some university as far away from Dexton as I could find. At times, I wondered if my body was just trying to keep up with my future, aggressive in every way.

"What's that supposed to mean?" Drake asked.

"It means that if you two spent more time finding work than fucking around, then maybe we could afford something nice instead of dragging it down the street."

They glanced at each other as if outed at last.

Dad never left the house anymore, so Drake and I hardly

had a solitary second together. Both of us just kept waiting on our fathers, hoping someday they'd come around and take us away from this land with no sign of water in sight.

"I don't know what you're talking about," Dad said, a cigarette hanging from his lip. They kept a fresh carton in the fridge. The air was constantly filled with a thin haze.

"I'm *sure* you don't," I said, standing for punctuation before stomping down the hall.

At night I took cold baths to keep me from running hot. Underwater, my skin all puckered, I'd picture Drake's stare. Like him witnessing these changes in me would somehow prove their happening. As if his showing up was a way to remind me things moved on—or maybe just stayed the same. It was similar to when I looked in the mirror and saw shades of both my parents: their soft features, the square fit of their shoulders, a bit of thickness about the frame. My reflection merely a shadowed attempt at imitation, like when you combine two pure forms of a chemical and only end up with a diluted replica of the former—a copy of a photocopy. How they were able to work their looks to get exactly what they wanted seemed beyond me.

Only when I wrapped the rest of me up in a towel and looked in the glass would my own face finally come into focus. I'd imagine Drake's sky-eyes taking me in. Then I'd think about what our first time together would be like. And though ridiculous, part of me hoped when we made love, naked and tangled in his hair, we wouldn't actually have to touch. There wouldn't even be kissing. In fact, maybe he wouldn't get hard like guys at school, the biker boys at the pumps. Twins weren't like that. Instead, we'd be lovers without the longing. Isn't that what true love was really supposed to be, after all: people in need without all that unnecessary neediness?

***

In August, sleep is miracle enough with the air smothering you like a quilt. Some nights I'd wake suffocating, a small dream twisted in the back of my mind like twine. I often dreamt of Drake—out in the shed and snoring as if under the spell of a gentle drug—until last night when I woke with a start. It felt as if something had been put back out of place. A lock left unlatched; a candle left to burn. But in the kitchen, dishes still sat in the sink, empties rested on the table. Outside, as I neared the noiseless shed, the sun peeked over the horizon, making the world look dusky and new. I wondered if this was it. The moment right before the moment I'd join with the only boy I'd ever found familiar—a brother without family or memory or any of those other obligations. I pictured Drake on the other side of the wall, drenched in sweat, troubled by the same dreams.

But inside, his cot was empty. My heart went limp, thinking it'd happened again.

What was it with this family where even a replacement part had the urge to leave without a word? No forwarding address. Just another unspoken goodbye. Back inside, the trailer felt hollow except for the dust that got into every crevice. I crossed my arms. Sometimes I couldn't even feel my own heartbeat through all that extra baggage. Where did it all come from, the sudden stuff that grew inside you until it couldn't be ignored, or contained, anymore?

Then I heard it.

Recently, nights had been filled with sad sounds coming from Dad's room. They weren't strong cries. Just small moans—strange in their slightness. I always thought he was just sniveling in his sleep. But tonight when I opened the door, despite the dark, it was easy to tell it wasn't weeping. These were living noises. Desperation had never had such a distinct timbre, a clear-cut quality that could only be created by two things turning into one. I wanted to slam the door but instead stood there, watching those frayed black braids wrestle a man's desire. It didn't look beautiful or satisfying. It looked danger-ous, almost brutal. Cruel in the way they moved, like a thirst turned vicious—a useless craving that no wish could ever fully quench.

Outside, the damp air tasted good for once. I picked up the basketball, its rubber worn down and air slightly flat. But oth-erwise it felt whole in my hands as I dribbled it against the dirt.

I wondered how long it'd been going on. But then there was the way they looked at one another, the way they were always smiling. All in all, it didn't seem like much of a conspir-acy. Their caution so evident it wasn't even worth the whis-pering.

Then, within a few minutes, the front door opened and a clump of dreads slunk out.

I shot a jumper, watched the silent swish of a net-less rim—but when the ball hit the dirt, Drake froze in place, as if he couldn't be seen as long as he didn't move.

"Too hot to sleep, isn't it?" I said, giving him a little grin. "How was *your* night?"

"Still tired."

"I bet." I rolled the ball on my fingertip, but it didn't last long before toppling.

Drake raised a brow, acting as if nothing happened. Like I was going to be that child left out of the family secret, kept in the dark until the lie got buried too deep for anyone to see.

He grabbed the ball and threw it in the air, missing by a mile. "Guess it's not my game."

I fetched the ball, gave it a bounce. "What *is* your game, exactly?"

"What do you want from me?" Drake asked, crossing his

arms. "It's like you're waiting for me to do something. But I don't have anything. Understand? Nothing."

I drilled another shot, rebounded, and passed him the ball. But he didn't move, letting himself get hit. He simply stood there, stock-still, as if holding his breath just to prove he could.

I picked up the ball again. "C'mon. Shoot it."

I threw it as hard as I could, the sound like a hammer strike against his skin.

Drake watched the ball roll to a stop. Then, before walking away, he shook his head and said, "Why is it people who have something never understand about nothing?"

I sat at the kitchen table wondering if Mom would've been on to them from the start. Or possibly knew all along. Maybe it's why she wanted me to keep Dad around in the first place: so I wouldn't have to worry about the typical clutter that came with men and their messes. It wasn't true, of course. But at the same time, when I imagined my mom's face on her deathbed, drifting off without even a daughter's love to keep her company, I knew some families could do a lot worse.

At noon, Dad emerged without a shirt, hair spiked with sleep. "How you doing, honey?"

"Thinking about Mom."

He whistled through his teeth. "Quite a woman. Tiny but tough as hell." He poured a cup and took a seat. "You ever meet your grandma?"

"Never knew I had one."

"My mom used to live right down the lane," he said, laughing to himself. "Also tough as hell."

"What happened to her?"

"Same as your mom, actually." Dad blew on his coffee and carefully took a sip. "Cancer."

"Did you come back just in time for her funeral too?"

He swallowed hard, a smile stuck on his face. "Got something on your mind, do you?"

"Know what happens next week?" He scrunched his brow like it was a prank, a small riddle from daughter to dad. But when I didn't stop my stare, letting him know it was a test and not a trick, the man simply shook his head, looking almost afraid of the answer. "It's my birthday."

The grin returned as he raised his mug. "Well, happy soon-to-be-birthday, honey."

"Know how old I'll be?" He shut his eyes, as if to do the math, until it went on a little too long. And though I knew the hazards of bringing up the past, knew the dead ends they shaped, I went ahead and asked anyway. "Did you even know I existed? Before you left?"

"What are you talking about? You were a beautiful baby." He studied his mug, tapped a finger against its rim. "Despite what you think, I did your mom a favor. I wasn't much good for her. So we had our time together and that was that."

I waited for him to continue, to come out with the truth for once. Instead he just sat back and drank his coffee.

"But I wonder what it would've been like if we'd had *our* time together."

"Honey," he said, "we're having it now, right?"

"Yeah. But where the hell have you been these last seventeen years?"

When my father finally looked my way, his smile was replaced by that same old squint, like I was giving off too much light. "What can I tell you? It is what it is."

"What kind of answer is that?" I asked, not quite sure what I wanted from him. If any kind of answer would've been the right one. Except my question only served to make him stand up and go back to bed—but not before telling me again how much I was like my mother.

Drake sat on the porch all morning, not talking to me. I had to be at work soon, but for now I lay in our pool wearing my bikini, trying to think of something that'd make him speak.

"He'll be leaving soon," I said, leaning back in the water. "Had a place to rest his head, but things are getting a little tight. And he'll make plans. Without us."

I slowly reached back and unclasped my top, letting my body breathe in the air.

"But *you* don't have to go, you know."

He didn't move, trying not to look. Except, when I finally captured his gaze, all he did was shut his eyes and say, "Hannah, we're trying to make this easy on you."

And it was only when I caught sight of my father's face staring from the kitchen window that I knew plans had already been made. I sat there, half-naked in a plastic kiddie pool, and saw how laughable I must've looked: like a cartoon of a girl that didn't quite make sense.

I covered up with a towel. "You don't have to do that."

Though, as I walked by, my hand couldn't resist running through his thick hair once more, as if telling him it was, at last, time to leave.

Dad met me at the door, almost resembling the man who first walked into our house: clean-shaven and soaked in smell-good, a saddlebag at his feet.

"Where are you going?" I asked.

"I've things to take care of." But there was that unsure look about his face again, as if he didn't know where to put his eyes. And it became clear this wasn't any trip—it was a getaway.

I pulled the towel tighter around myself. "Can I come with you?"

Dad went to touch my arm, but hesitated. His hand hovered there—not certain whether to shove me or hug me, give a lecture or not say a word—until finally he pulled back and shouldered his bag. "You'll be better off without us."

"Us?" At first, the word felt promising, almost pretty. Like maybe it meant me, and somehow Mom as well, until I saw it only included him. And a lost boy with no strings attached.

"You come from strong stock."

"I guess I didn't get that from you." I tried to think of what Mom would do—laugh in his face, curse his name—when all I wanted was to throw my arms around him, bury my face into his leather vest, smell the raw warmth living there. But I didn't do that either.

"You're right about that," he said. "But you'll be just fine."

"Will I?"

Dad stopped at the door, the handle already in his hand. "Well, then you'll make do."

I stood on the porch as he helped Drake onto his bike. Dad gave it a kick, the engine flaring to life, as he said something to the boy holding onto his back. Drake shrugged and gave me a shy wave, as if confused by what the goodbye was all about, until they tore down the road, mindlessly spraying gravel left and right, to and fro.

Tonight the bath is cold. The sun and heat won't rub off. It sits on my skin, radiating from within, a place that can't be touched with water. Drops drip from the faucet, the porcelain rough with scum. I shut my eyes and think about what's missing. Though everything's here—the couch, a poor excuse for a rug—tonight, when I walked in after work, the one thing I wasn't ready for was the silence, as if the very air had been stolen from beneath me.

I picture two men on the back of a bike, strangers who found a way out and took it for what it was worth, even if it wasn't much. I try to find comfort there. That maybe I had a hand in making a new something from out of all this nothing.

As I stare at the sad sight of myself, I wonder what Mom would think. How the one thing that lured people into her life

21

had failed her own daughter. Like that first day Dad showed, and she almost looked alive again. She didn't even seem sick, slipping her slight body into my old clothes that'd become too small for me but now fit her like a quick road to recovery. Until one night, she pulled me close, took out a tube of lipstick, and told me to pucker up. To be a good girl. To not make the same mistake and never let him go. But before she had a chance to improve a thing about me, I pushed her away and walked from the room—though not before telling my mom desperation wasn't a good look on her. Still, when she passed away that very night, with only an old lover by her side, I knew I'd be asking him to stay. If simply as a way to say sorry.

But this is better. Put out to pasture—a story we both understood all too well around here.

In fact, next week, I'll be the same age my mother was when she had me. So, tonight, I'll lie in her bed and share the same sleep, sweating out the dreams.

I try to guess about them, those dreams. How they often seem so real but so wrong: a duplicate of a place where you're not entirely you but close to it. Like an out-of-body experience between two worlds, both of which you can see, yet still can't quite grasp.

But first, before sleep, comes the heat. It's something to depend upon around here. The one thing you can rely on when everything else seems to melt and burn away.

SMOKED

Ever since Heath got off the bus, it'd been a blur of alcohol, two solid days of it. Gloria Dempsey, his high school girlfriend, followed his platoon everywhere but refused to drink. Each time a bartender bought a round on the house, she'd look at him as if the camo fatigues worked just as well over here as over there. Sinclair, their squad leader, sliced a hand on broken glass. Dunbar, a giant farm boy, picked a fight that ended with a shiner. Carver literally lost his shirt at The Lunch Box, a strip club outside the city limits of Dexton, and walked half-naked down Main Street.

That second night, Gloria half-carried Heath to the basement bedroom of his parents' house. He was close to passing out when she appeared from the bathroom, wearing only underwear and no longer looking young. In the year since he'd been deployed, the girl he once knew had shed the baby fat and vanished into a body full of strict angles.

Gloria crossed her thin arms and kicked the mattress. He tried to pry open his eyes.

Then she whispered something and gently pressed her bare foot into his crotch.

He wanted to ask what she said. What she wanted from

him. The only words that made any sense tonight came in the form of questions. He quietly told her, "Don't?"

She smiled and sat on his lap. Each edge of her dug into him, like holding a skeleton. She tugged at his ear with her teeth. Her skin smelled sharp as spice. He wanted to never let go.

They woke on separate sides of the bed, the air like a tomb. Dust coated each surface. Gloria's eyes were open, but he couldn't bring himself to touch her. Before coming back, the psych consult said to take it easy on fooling around. And now here they were, awake and alone for the first time. Instead, Heath touched the sheets they had slept upon. He'd never felt anything so clean.

His limbs ached. The alcohol hadn't left his blood yet. He promised himself to quit smoking, a habit picked up during Basic, but the cravings had set in. All he could remember from last night was Gloria trying to kiss him, here then there, places he wasn't used to being handled. She told him to lay back, relax. He told her to go away, giving her a soft shove.

They'd never shared an entire night together. He wondered if her dad was the type to stay up, sick with worry. But he'd never met the man so couldn't know for sure. He only knew her dad was a professor at Northern Community College. That it was just the two of them living in a big house in Bridger. Gloria didn't talk about her mom. Or why she left their family. But it maybe explained why his girlfriend was the way she was. Gloria Dempsey: good grades, student council, cheerleader. Everything a girl was supposed to be. Her favorite book was the Bible. She loved art and poetry. Over the last year, Heath dreamt of her heart-shaped face. The muscled curve of her body. When his platoon saw her photo, they said, "Girl next door. Best kind of lay."

But Gloria also dreamt of things, like marriage. She wanted ten children. There was talk of universities, graduate school.

And though these things sounded nice, they also felt too much like dreams, a word that made him cautious. Heath Sawyer was C-average, all around. At Roosevelt High, he didn't go out for football. Rarely went to class. Never even bothered filling out college applications. So at the start of their senior year, when he saw the Twin Towers fall, over and again on TV, he went to the recruitment office and enlisted the next day. And when Gloria asked why, he couldn't say exactly. It was just something he needed to do.

At first she cried. Then she yelled, said not to expect her to stick around, just waiting for life to begin. Heath felt a certain relief in the ultimatum, offered her his signing bonus as a way to jumpstart that life. But a year later, not long into his deployment, she wrote about enrolling at NCC—until his return. He chose to ignore it. What could he do halfway around the world?

Overseas, each of her e-mails ended with *I love you* as if reciting a prayer. But now, two days home, they still hadn't said it aloud, the word sounding too strange. Plus, it felt like she'd somehow grown, her height seeming to equal his. Her shock of yellow hair had turned the color of wheat. And her face looked carved down, the eyes hollowed out. She was still beautiful. More so, in fact. Except, even in the way she smelled now—close to raw, almost animal—lay a power he wasn't sure what to do with. In bed, her stillness was like a nerve he didn't dare disturb.

Heath opened the curtains. Light fell through the window-wells lining the basement.

"Close it, please." She hid her eyes beneath the sheets. "It hurts."

He did as he was told, accustomed to following orders.

"It's a beautiful day," he said, though from the depths of the cellar it was difficult to say. Gloria didn't move when he sat next to her. "Did you know you snore in your sleep?"

Heath kissed the blanket shrouding her face when she said,

"Did you know you scream?"

He'd fantasized about this moment. But now that it'd arrived, it wasn't as he'd imagined.

"I should see my folks. They've been waiting."

Gloria slipped the sheet off her face. "So have I."

He put a finger to her lips, startled by their coarseness, and said he was sorry. But when she closed her eyes again, he knew—as he somehow always knew—that it simply wasn't enough.

When Heath entered the kitchen, his father quickly dropped the paper, his mother already out of her chair. Last fall, when he got on the bus, his mom wouldn't stop smiling. Her grin— tight-lipped, pretty, proud—was like the sand that got into everything. A grain of grit he held in his gut day in, day out. But this week, at the homecoming, when his mother waved a little flag like a wand, her smile finally broke. She hugged him until he told her, "I'm okay."

"Maybe I'm not." Then she'd laughed as if it was some inside joke.

But this morning the smile was back. "You hungry? Your first meal should be special."

This year, though it was the little things he'd missed most— walking around in socks, lying on a bed—it'd all been simpler. He didn't have to make decisions about clothes or sleep. These choices were given to him like a gift. But now it felt crucial he not make a mistake.

"Eggs." His legs jittered beneath the kitchen table. "It'd be nice to have some real eggs."

Her eyes widened with gratitude. "Yes, sir."

He grabbed the Classifieds though he knew it was full of overqualified jobs. He'd considered community college but sitting at a desk and listening to lectures just felt childish now.

"Cubs are in trouble this year." His dad handed over the sports section. It was strange to live in a state surrounded by pro teams. And since Iowa lay in between, loyalties were divided. Still, it was fitting that Dexton claimed the team famous for being so close but never quite there.

"What's new?"

His dad laughed. "Some things remain the same. They pulled one out yesterday, too late in the season to count. It's for the best, though. It only hurts when you get your hopes up."

But before Heath could say anything about hope, before he could get a word out about the slippery concept of change, the fridge slammed shut, making him jump to his feet.

"We're out of eggs."

"That's okay, Mom."

"It's not okay." She'd already grabbed her purse. "I'll be right back."

"Just stop. Please. I don't need eggs."

"What can we do then?" his mother asked, clutching her car keys.

And though there were several answers to the question, nobody said anything, each of them unsure of what to do next, until his father told him, "You always have a place at the shop."

Heath sat back down and nodded, knowing his dad didn't need any extra help. He owned a small hardware store that used to deal with local construction crews. But now that the county had voted for the newly proposed Highway 20 to be built through Bridger instead of Dexton, his dad would be lucky to sell the occasional nut and bolt to a do-it-yourselfer.

"Or at least I know contractors who need help," his dad said. "If you're looking for something temporary. I mean, it's the least we can do for you after all you've done for us."

Heath heard it often. When in fatigues, strangers shook his hand as if asking forgiveness. As if they had something in common. Like he could get away with anything. At least for a time.

"Sure," Heath said with a sigh. "Something temporary sounds nice."

***

When they'd first stepped off the bird into all that sand, SFC Brian Hills gave a salute and said to start digging. They'd been assigned Delta camp, a few miles south of Kandahar, a region rife with enemy fire. But they'd come two weeks into Ramadan, so for a while they lived in relative quiet, the desert seeming all the more dangerous for it. In this spare time, it was basic training all over again. They were smoked by superior officers—sandbagging and excavating.

On patrol, they drove the same two-mile stretch of blacktop cutting through the land like an oil slick. Hills was the first to inspect the objects along the road, not so much because he didn't have faith in them but because he didn't have faith in anyone. Sometimes it was just a tin can. Sometimes it was a pile of stones atop a metal plate with wires. They'd detonate it, the fifty-pound charge lingering in their bones until the next day, when the same traps would be waiting in the same places. Each time a civilian came near—a child begging for candy, a man talking on a cell phone—Heath wondered if they would be the next thing to be set off.

Hills encouraged them to write letters to help focus on why they were there, all of which felt absurd. Most talked about the weather. The lack of things to look at. How they just drove around almost searching for a trouble that couldn't be found. Until the holiday ended and, as on every patrol, the Humvee broke down in broad daylight. They got out and did an IED inspection. Nobody spoke, the silence forcing them to stay frosty and alert. Under the hood they replaced a hose. Then a blast ripped open the air. Dunbar shot at the horizon. Sinclair called in their location. Heath helped Martinez take cover under the Humvee. Then, as fast as it began, it ended. He thought firefights would last longer, but within seconds the quiet came back with Hills writhing on the ground, a shard of shrapnel impaled into the orbit of his right eye.

Timed RPGs, they were told later. Like a clock radio, they were set in advance. The enemy was already miles away. Returning fire had been pointless. Their heads ached for days. Their new leader was flown home without a goodbye and only half his vision.

For weeks, Heath kept wondering how to put these things in a letter.

Gloria picked him up in her father's old Buick Regal. It smelled of smoke and wintergreen—the air fresheners not quite covering up the scent. Heath wondered when she started smoking; if it was her cigarettes or someone else's.

"I can't believe you still have this thing."

He remembered the car as huge, too big for such a little girl. But now, like everything else, it felt cramped. In the desert, they talked about the Real World: holiday dinners and easy chairs and bathtubs you could sit in. Everything was oversized in scale, but now seemed so small. Buildings in each direction. Cars all over the road. Even his own house felt full of walls.

"You bet." Tonight, Gloria looked happy, smiling with all her teeth. It made him breathe a bit easier. "The old make-out machine."

They both tried to laugh.

"What movie do you want to see?" she asked. "There's an action film playing."

"No." It was the kind of movie she never wanted to see, the sort of movie he used to love. But now the thought of noise made him nervous. "I mean, what do *you* want to see?"

"I don't know." She pulled up to a stop sign. "You usually chose the movie."

"I'm sorry," he said. It was a phrase she seemed to bring out of him lately.

"It made things easier." She kept her foot on the brake, as if forgetting to move forward. "You were the one thing in my life that made it simple for once. I loved that about you."

"And then I went and made it all complicated."

"No." Gloria shook her head. "I did."

He wasn't sure how, but nodded anyway because it felt like something a boyfriend did. Or something he used to do—apparently avoiding problems was part of his charm. But when she reached for his hand, Heath quickly fingered the air fresheners that hung from the rearview mirror, along with her graduation tassels—*Class of 2002*—a ceremony he skipped since they had to report for boot camp in Georgia before summer began. "Sorry I missed your commencement."

"It was yours too," she laughed. "They even called your name."

"But I should have been there—to hear your name." She looked ready to cry until Heath clapped his hands, making Gloria flinch. "So we going to see a movie or what?"

"Yeah," she said, shifting the car into Park only to shake her head and pull it back into Drive. She stepped on the gas too hard, forcing them to lurch through the intersection.

"How about a romance," he said. "Is that something you'd like?" But when she simply shrugged and stared off down the road, he wasn't sure it was the right question at all.

The next night, his old high school friends invited him to The Tap. It felt good to be asked along until he realized it was only because of his military ID, which was better than any fake. The room was full of men who'd gotten off work or had never gone in the first place. And somehow over the last year these boys that Heath had thought of as the best kind of friends had turned into the worst kind of townies, making Dexton seem all the more small. They spoke of baseball and jobs and girls. As if they'd put the conversation on pause, resuming right where he'd left off. They sounded like something on TV. He couldn't believe people still talked this way.

Garrett Miller—a kid who, senior year, served time for possession, but not before getting an underage girl pregnant—took a deep drag on his smoke and asked, "Kill anyone over there?"

Heath couldn't believe Garrett was a year younger and also a father now. He wanted to ask him how he did it. How a high school loser with a criminal record could get out of jail and simply move on like nothing happened. Why someone like him deserved such a normal life.

Instead, Heath gazed into his mug and said, "It's hard to tell what I did over there."

They laughed until Garrett said, "And Gloria? You guys getting along all right?"

Heath was curious if they'd think it strange that they'd barely talked, much less kissed. "She got skinny. But it's good. Just different, I guess."

These friends with their acne scars and yellow teeth exchanged a curious look. Then they slowly sipped at their beer. The jukebox's speakers suddenly went quiet between songs.

"What's going on?" Heath asked, though he had an idea. It wasn't anything specific, but over the year Gloria's letters had changed. At the start, her messages spoke of pride and pining. But eventually they only talked about classes and how this town was getting the best of her. They still began and ended with love but her words became distant, full of less, and at some point read as if assigned to her for homework, like she was trying not to say something.

"Nothing's different around here, man," Garrett said, anxiously stabbing out his cigarette. "More things change, the more they stay the same, right?"

Heath smacked the table, spilling his mug. "The fuck do you know about any of that?"

Some took a drink, others looked at the wall, each waiting for music to fill in the space they'd accidentally created.

***

After his friends left, Heath considered calling Gloria. They hadn't seen each other today and it felt like the thing to do. Instead, he bellied up to the bar and showed his military ID. He was offered another free drink but insisted on paying when a man next to him said, "You a vet, too?"

He'd had this conversation before: guys sparking up ancient memories of their own wars. For WWII, they'd talk medals and funerals. Vietnam, it'd be whorehouses and limbs left behind.

Either way, the stories always felt inflated.

"I was there, you know." The man finished off his drink. "Desert Storm."

"Is that so?" Part of him wanted to laugh. But instead he asked, "What was your MO?"

"Expendable." The man jabbed a cigarette into his mouth. "First Class."

Heath handed over a book of matches, but the vet waved it away.

"I quit," he said. "Just can't help holding one in my hand."

"We lost someone," Heath said. "Came back in pieces. Hit them pretty hard over here."

"Happens all the time, right?" The stranger took an imaginary pull of smoke.

"Not if you know what you're doing." Heath held the beer to his mouth then put it back on the bar and pointed to the man's cigarettes. "Can I have one?"

The man raised his eyebrows and shrugged. "Had the same pack for years."

Heath plucked one out, the filter mushy between his fingers. "Like a souvenir."

"Something like that."

They sat together and puffed on the unlit tips. But the stale taste of dry tobacco only made Heath crave the feel of fire, his mouth left watering for the real thing.

***

A knock came from his window. Gloria crawled into his bedroom smelling of smoke. She wore old cheerleading shorts, at first resembling her former self, until his girlfriend's face fell into the light. Her hair was buzzed on one side. A swath of bangs draped the other half, covering her left eye. She looked ready to apologize until she asked, "Do you like it?"

"It's interesting."

They lay in his bed at arm's length until she asked if he wanted to talk about it.

"Talk about what?"

"They shut down the e-mail afterwards. For days I was out of my mind. Couldn't sleep. Nobody to talk to."

"Nobody?"

"You're the only person left that I could talk to about it." She rested her shaved head upon his chest. "Kind of funny, huh?"

He tried to stroke her hair, but it felt too close to the skin. "I guess."

"Then I got the news. I was so happy. Does that make me a bad person?"

"No. It makes me a lucky person."

She turned to face him, her nose less than an inch away from his. "I went to the funeral."

"You didn't even know Martinez."

"It was a closed casket. The twenty-one guns were terrifying. Why do that to people?"

"You get used to it."

"Were you there?" she asked. "When it happened?"

"Is there something you want to tell me?" He sensed the heat of her body. Her musty clothes sparked a hunger in his gut. "Don't explain. Just tell me."

In the dark, he wasn't sure if her eyes were open. She cradled his cheeks, her fingers so warm they burned his face. He could feel her lips move when she whispered, "I love you."

He wanted to ask questions. He wanted to say the same of her. He wanted to touch each part of her with himself. But instead he simply said "Thank you" to keep from crying in her hands.

The letters became easier as the mission became clearer—in strategy and in their minds. At night he thought of Gloria writing a paper, his parents making car payments, and felt sorry for them. In his last letter, the one they carried on their persons at all times, he apologized for making them suffer his decision to enlist. He wrote of the enemy. How he had more in common with them than anyone back home. How death wasn't scary, was almost easy to accept, due to this fact.

He ended the letter by praying for God to forgive him.

He pleaded for his family to take comfort in these thoughts.

He asked Gloria to someday let her ten children know about him—that despite never being able to meet these unborn girls and boys he loved them more than they could imagine.

And, lastly, he hoped nobody would ever have to read these final words.

Before the parades, Sinclair gave everyone his contacts. It was his second tour. He warned about homecomings. In fact, he pulled Heath aside that night, saying to be especially careful. At the time, Heath didn't know what it meant, but now here he was in the man's apartment after driving across three counties. It was stranger still to see a superior in civilian clothes, a four-day beard clinging to his face. His fridge held only a pizza box, a case of beer. The living room was nearly vacant: two folding chairs facing a tiny TV. The Cubs played with the sound muted.

"Sleeping okay?" Sinclair asked.

"Aren't you?" They both grinned and drank their beer.

"I don't even have a bed. Slept better in the Suck."

Heath gently squeezed his aluminum can. "I think my girl may have found a Jody."

"Jody, huh?" Sinclair gave him a wink. "Good for her."

"Sir, you're an asshole."

"You know, that's your big problem."

"What's my big problem?"

"What did you expect? The world to stop? All anyone knows to do is put a sticker on their bumper. Then they can go back to watching the latest celebrity sex tape."

He wanted to tell Sinclair about this afternoon at the grocery store. The lines of cereal boxes that went on forever, so perfectly stacked and ready to eat, made Heath clutch the cart. People walked around him as if he were in the way, baskets filled with enough food to feed an entire Afghan village. The moment felt so mundane, so matter-of-fact, he came close to crying.

Another batter popped out to end the inning.

"Losing streak continues." Sinclair slapped a bandaged hand against his leg. He said he couldn't recall how the injury occurred, though their first night home Heath had witnessed him punching a restroom mirror. Afterward, Sinclair had studied the gash as if amazed by the sight.

"Heard from anyone else?"

"Had to bail out Dunbar," Sinclair said. "Drunk and still fighting. Didn't even know where he was when I picked him up. They let him off, of course."

"Is it strange that I'm jealous?" Heath asked.

"Of what?"

"At least he's doing something about it."

"It's not strange." Sinclair gestured at the empty room. "Look at the alternative."

***

The campus was overrun by students. They strolled between buildings and filled the sidewalks. Talked about parties and professors. Indian summer had lasted too long already, the grass around the college still green in October. Girls stripped down to tank tops, their skin brown and shiny. Though everyone was his age, they all looked like children: young and safe and oblivious. He wanted to take comfort in this fact, but the mass of bodies only made his head hurt.

Heath searched the grounds, thinking of things to say. He'd taken his lunch break to come here, and on the way had rehearsed words about love and fresh starts. But now, as he caught a glimpse of Gloria talking with Garrett Miller, both of them looking so sad for the other, all those things he'd wanted to say felt naïve and without cause. She wore ripped jeans and no makeup, her stick-thin body practically swimming in an oversized T-shirt. So unlike the Gloria he knew. The one who wore barrettes and lip gloss and teared up when speaking of a mother's absence. Heath had wanted to love her from that moment, protect her every day. Except now, seeing her half-shaved head through the crowd, he wasn't sure he'd done either.

Heath curled his fists, fingernails digging into his palm. He imagined the pleasure of a first strike. Then tried to recall his final evaluation. How the psych doc advised him to picture his blood pressure dropping point by point. That there was power in granting people a little mercy.

However, as he approached, Gloria's face went white. "What are you doing here?"

"Hey, man." Garrett gradually backed away. "How you doing?"

Heath didn't look at him, unsure of what'd happen if he did. "Came to give you a ride."

Gloria shrugged, offering Garrett an apologetic smile. "I'll talk to you later, okay?"

"He won't have time for that. Right, Garrett?" Heath cleared his throat. "Don't you have some jailbait to knock up some-where?"

Before Garrett could answer, Heath grabbed Gloria's wrist and led her across campus. They didn't say anything until in the parking lot, standing on opposite sides of his work truck.

"I can't believe you. Why did you say that?"

"Say what? It's true, isn't it?"

Gloria crossed her arms. "Are you following me?"

"Should I be?"

"This isn't an interrogation." She hugged her books. "Maybe you could talk to someone."

"I talk to you."

"Someone else. Someone qualified."

"I bet Garrett is a great listener, right?" When he slid behind the wheel, Gloria wasn't next to him. "Listen, stop being so smart and get your ass in the car."

Instead, she poked her head through the passenger window and said, "I drove myself."

Watching her walk away, another silly schoolgirl lost in the crowd, he wanted to punch something. Or run someone over—if only to show them what it felt like to not see it coming.

They signed up together. Carver graduated a year before. Dunbar was even older but still hung out with the football team. Martinez was from somewhere across the state. At first, the kid never opened his mouth. Then, when he did finally talk, the words came out garbled, thick with an accent. As if he knew the vocabulary but wasn't sure how to use it. They smoked him for his dark skin, his silence, the way he whistled when he worked. He'd simply smile back as if begging to be liked. Until they were deployed, and communication became so impos-sible they resorted to hand signals on patrol. Under fire, the only way to get Martinez out of harm's way was to take his arm and pull him to safety. After Hills left, they all took turns sighting objects along the roadside—except Martinez, who had no idea what to look for or how to find it without putting them at risk. So back at base, they'd make him do shit-work, telling him ditch-digging was in his blood.

This was why Heath sent Martinez to go fetch water.

It'd been a grueling afternoon: no detected IEDs, a failed mission, which only meant they were still out there, waiting for them. Martinez sat in the Humvee, not paying attention, as always. But today it was his whistling—like the shrill howl of desert wind, coming around corners and over dunes—that shattered Heath's nerve. And when the nerve is gone, so is your will. And when that leaves, you might as well zip up your own body bag. So back at camp, he ordered Martinez to round up water for the *real* soldiers like some kind of fresh fish right off the bus. Though at first Martinez gave mean glares and unsure glances, eventually he did as he was told. But when he stepped into the stock room, the building went up in a cloud of smoke. Then the entryway collapsed, followed by that well-known feeling of losing one's hold on the earth.

A pressure-mounted plate lay buried under the doorway, a threshold they'd all crossed countless times. Except today Martinez didn't have time to put down his gear, adding another hundred pounds to his weight. Everyone wondered why they hadn't noticed it before. How it'd gotten there in the first place. Had it been there all along? And why was Martinez in such a rush that he wouldn't at least put down his load before satisfying his thirst?

Work reminded Heath of the desert: rolling over rubble, taking orders from fat-bellied bosses, driving around with no clear mission in mind. An apartment complex was being erected, but since he'd been given the job as a favor to his father, Heath mostly sat in the work truck and watched day laborers nail studs while listening to Mexican radio. He read the paper, sipped coffee, snuck in naps before lunch. But today, after driving back from NCC, the foreman tapped his window and spoke slowly, as if carefully choosing his words. "We need you today."

The air felt wet as he followed the foreman—a guy named Rick who was only a few years older—into the barebones structure. They stood in front of a small hole above the kitchen sink. "Forecast is calling for more rain. Need to get these openings closed."

"Yes, sir." His voice was crisp, the words familiar in his mouth.

"Thought we'd start with something small." Rick pointed to the window on the floor. "See how you handle it."

Heath wanted to laugh but knew better. "I can handle it."

"That's what I like to hear."

Rick walked away, leaving Heath to stare at the tiny void in the wall.

Each step was easy enough: mount the casement, staple vapor barrier, nail the flashings. Except afterward, though it felt finished, once he pushed in the insulation and fitted the trim, Heath noticed cracks of light around the edge. He started over, retraced the procedure, but when Rick finally inspected his work, the window wouldn't open. "Did you level it?"

Heath felt flushed and damp, sweat dripping from his hair. "Why wouldn't it be level?"

"Then I'm assuming you didn't shim it."

"You shouldn't need to, right? If the work around it isn't shoddy?"

The foreman sighed. "Do it again. Get someone to help you this time."

"I don't need any help. Least of all from some spic."

Rick looked right, then left. The men nearby simply kept hammering and measuring.

"See," Heath said. "They don't even understand us."

"Why don't you go back to the truck?"

"Fine with me." He dropped the caulk gun into the sink. It clattered against the metal. Everyone stopped their work, staring at him like a criminal. "What the hell are you looking at?"

Outside, he stared at the window. Saw its uneven seams, the crooked lines. Then felt heat enter his hands as he picked up a stray hammer and threw it at the glass with all his strength.

He'd been driving around for hours in the company truck, circling the sea of cornfields.

The humidity was stifling, which didn't help his nerves. He'd tried to call Sinclair, but there was no answer. And Carver's number was no longer in service. But then he remembered Dunbar, who lived alone in an old farmhouse out by the county line. It'd been in his family for generations and he'd used his sign-up pay to get it out of hock. It was all he talked about at the Beach, saying he'd fix it up right, maybe stake out a bit more land for himself. But when Heath parked in the gravel driveway, the place looked boarded up, the yard bursting with weeds.

Through the torn screen door hung an Eviction Notice: weather-beaten and barely legible. Heath knocked but was about to give up when the door cracked open. And there stood Dunbar with a swollen eye, fresh stitches poking from his face like barbwire.

"Get the hell out of here," he said, flashing an unfolded KA-BAR through the gap.

"Hey, it's just me."

Dunbar shielded his eyes against the day and smiled. "Thought you were the bank again."

They sat on the porch, Dunbar in dirty fatigues, his boots covered in manure and mud.

"What happened to your face?"

Dunbar cracked a beer, the sharp pop bringing Heath to his feet again.

"Went to a party," he said. "Didn't take long for some punk to start talking shit."

"Heard you got arrested."

"Can't remember much." Dunbar dug the small blade of his pocketknife under his nails, cleaning them. "Said I broke his nose. Nothing new. But I guess it felt different this time."

The rows of corn made Heath uneasy. He studied the stalks swaying in the breeze; perfect cover for someone to hide behind. "Have you visited Martinez's grave?"

"Been meaning to." Dunbar took a sip and laughed. "It's not Martinez, anyway. Just a bunch of spare parts, you know. Fucked up way to go."

"I wonder what he was like. Over here."

"Same as anybody." Dunbar walked over to his front door and ripped down the Eviction Notice. "Bet his parents got a big fat check, though."

"They deserve it. Better than just a folded-up flag."

"You remember that day when..." Dunbar worked his mouth as if tasting what he wanted to say. Heath waited for the words, hoping they weren't just another punchline, another war story about who they used to be. Instead, Dunbar crushed his can and threw it into the yard. Then he gently smoothed the notice against the porch rail as if getting ready to read it out loud.

"Have you heard anything about our orders?" Heath asked.

"You think we're going back?"

"I don't know. Maybe. I hope so."

"No shit." Dunbar touched his black eye and flinched. "So how's that girl of yours?"

"She grew up. Found somebody more worth her while, I guess."

They sat in silence for a second until Dunbar suddenly stabbed the notice into the railing. Heath jumped and stared at the KA-BAR sticking out of the wood like a sundial.

"Hey, you want to help me burn this place down?" Dunbar

grinned and slapped him on the back. "Just another thing worth more dead than alive."

In the dark, the apartment complex looked burnt-out. Piles of lumber and rolls of Tyvek littered the construction site. Stacks of brick sat like castles in the sand. The pressure in the atmosphere had dropped by small degrees all day, the air humming with energy.

Heat-lightning streaked the sky, illuminating the tarp that covered the window.

When he called Gloria, she answered by asking if he'd broken anything else, stolen another truck, done something stupid. His parents had phoned her, out of their minds with worry.

"Stop with the cross-examination," he said, telling her where to meet, if she still cared.

There was a brief pause, a small gasp, and then finally she agreed—no questions asked.

Heath turned on the radio, thumbed through the stations, but everything was full of static. He turned it off. The tarp over the kitchen window shook in the wind, rattling like a snake.

As the Buick pulled up, he got out of his truck. An icy rain clinked against their cars.

"What are we doing here?" she asked, cautiously making her way toward him.

"What do you mean we?"

She flung back her hair, revealing a shine in her eyes. "What's your problem?"

He stroked the side of her head. "Look at this, for Christ's sake."

"I knew you'd hate it."

"Is that why you did it? To prove a point?"

"I'm not the enemy, Heath. I didn't do anything to you."

"True." He pointed to the thin outline of her ribs. "It's like you're not even here at all."

"I don't like this place. Can we go now?"

"Want to see something funny?" Heath walked up the incline, mud clutching his shoes.

He ripped away the tarp, revealing the broken window like a magic trick. The jagged teeth of the glass gleamed in the night, lit up by the occasional flash of light. "Ugly, isn't it?"

Gloria came close, inspecting the damage. "Maybe you can still fix it. Tomorrow. Say you're sorry and that you'll fix it."

"Sounds simple enough, doesn't it."

Heath traced his finger along a shard of glass, the bite of it precise against his skin.

"What are you doing?" Gloria cringed and hugged her chest. "Doesn't that hurt?"

"Sometimes," he said, the blood already running down his finger. He exhaled, the sting satisfying for the moment.

"What am I supposed to do?" she whispered.

"Nothing." In the distance, tornado sirens began to howl. "You're not here, remember?"

The whites of her eyes widened. "This isn't funny."

"Then you should've left when you had the chance."

He took her hand, but she shrunk back and sucked in her breath. "Don't."

"Are you scared?"

She shook her head. Sirens wailed across town, their drone rising and falling on the wind.

When Heath went for her hand again, this time she let him take it. He guided her to the window, held her fingertip above the tip of glass. "Yeah, you're fucking terrified."

Instead of pulling away, a shadow of a smile crossed her face. "Aren't you?"

He loosened his grip, wanting to tell her all the ways there were to be afraid. But before he could start to explain what fear meant, what it was to be truly frightened of not being afraid, she gently grasped his wrist. Heath wanted to tell her to stop as she put his hand to her lips and lightly sucked at the wound. He felt his knees give. His heart slowed. Soon, he had to shut his eyes, wincing at the feel of her mouth, so warm, so soft, it almost hurt to touch it.

BIRMINGHAM HOUSE

1.

When Penny is alone with the new boy, when she asks him to empty his pockets, she makes sure the door stays open. Every time there's a new intake she's never sure what will be pulled out of the next kid's pants, the next girl's purse, each backpack full of last-minute possessions, random items packed in a hurry. The boy is named Carl. Penny has been told his mom can't handle him anymore. Something about threatening a teacher, bringing a weapon to school. Of course, it was just talk, empty words all bullies depend on. But it was enough to get him sent here.

Carl doesn't move, making Penny repeat herself. "Let's go. I'm waiting."

She shouldn't be alone with him. Male associates are supposed to register the boys, but they're short-staffed. The manager left for the day and the only other adult is outside, supervising Recreation, playing softball. The kids say Penny throws like a girl, which she supposes she does. Sometimes she wishes she were bigger, stocky, like a man. Then maybe boys like Carl wouldn't stare her down, biting their lips as if she were something sweet to taste.

The cinderblock walls of Birmingham House are yellowed with age. The carpet is bald from all those shoes treading back and forth. Everyone arrives with a story, but then, before you can even catch their name, they're gone. To the next facility, the next home, the next stop on their way through the system. In the past year that she's been a staffer at Birmingham House, Penny has never seen anyone return. She's still not sure if this is good or bad.

Carl is dressed in camouflage from head to toe, his hair cut high and tight. He stares at Penny for a full minute before she finally says, "We can do this the hard or easy way."

She's never sure what the hard way would be, since they can't touch the client. She could remove skill points, drop him a level—force extra chores. Other than this, she has little to bargain with. Boys tend to stop the tough-guy routine within the first few days. Girls are different. They come in crying: fragile things hiding in bed. But unlike guys, their anger never truly leaves them. They're quiet and hostile. Penny knows all about these things. How the rage can live with you for years, the wounds that never fully heal. It's part of the reason she's here.

But she also knows the trouble this kind of hurt can lead to.

When Carl slowly unbuckles his belt, Penny wonders if she'll have to call for help. Penny has never been attacked. Most kids aren't violent. Damaged maybe, but usually more difficult than dangerous. Sometimes she still feels sorry for them. Her first month on the job she pitied everybody, but lately she feels the humanity slipping away from her like sand through fingers. She came to help, but soon realized she was simply a substitute teacher. And all the kids know it.

"What are you doing?" she asks, on the verge of yelling for backup.

"You want this, don't you?"

She isn't sure if it's a question or a command until he

pulls the belt through the loops and offers it to her. "This isn't prison," Penny says. "Just empty your pockets."

He hands over the belt anyway, so she indulges him. But when Penny takes hold of it, he pulls the leather strap, bringing her to his chest. His breath is surprisingly sweet, the smell of mint enveloping her. She wants to run away, scream, but when he whispers, "Don't worry. You're safe," part of her believes him.

He puts both hands behind his head and says, "Ready for inspection."

Though it's against the rules, and her better judgment, Penny just wants to get this done. She slides her hands across his body, bends to feel around his black combat boots. Her heart heaves. Her skin slicks over. But still, it's almost a relief to finally touch one of the kids, see they're simply flesh and bone. That they're not as delicate as everyone thinks. That maybe she doesn't always have to worry about them breaking so easily under her watch.

Until she feels the hard bulge in Carl's pocket, a long outline pressing through the cloth.

"Getting warmer," he says.

She can feel the smile in his words as she reaches into his pants and pulls out a black knife. It's thin and collapsible and trembles in her hand.

"Busted." Carl throws his hands in the air, the smirk spreading across his face. "That's a KA-BAR. Army-issue. It was my dad's."

The knife is still warm from his body. She pinches it between her fingers, holding it in the air like a dead rat by its tail. "Well, it's mine now."

"C'mon." He gestures for her to come close, to stop playing around. "Don't be that way."

But when she drops the knife into a plastic bag, when he sees their game is over, that the test has failed, Carl drops his shit-eating grin. His body shakes. His face fills with blood.

"My father didn't die for this country so some government bitch can come and..." His breath has become ragged, almost panting, like some strange animal. "I have rights, you know."

Penny laughs, zipping the bag up tight. "Not here you don't."

2.

The windows unlock from the inside, so for weeks—between chores and Group, after school and before dinner—they've been hatching The Plan. A few months ago they hadn't thought it through. So when Katy lowered her little brother to the ground, hanging him over the windowsill, Penny had walked in on them, asking, "And where do you two think you're going?"

Nothing in this place goes unseen. There aren't security cameras or alarms, but that doesn't mean there aren't eyes around every corner, watching. So now there's no room for error. It'll have to be when the house is completely quiet. The night shift staffer starts her homework around midnight, two hours after curfew, and nods off around three. That's when they'll try again. Katy knows from rumors that float around the house that once the staff notices their absence, they'll lock the window behind them. This way, when escapees return, as they always do, no one can come back undetected. They'll be caught in the act and split up for sure. So this time, once they're gone, there's no turning back.

Of course, Penny's question was a good one. Where did they think they were going? The first attempt had no destination—they just wanted out. Together. The threat of separation loomed before them each day as "the powers that be" decided what was best for them. But they'd been through too much, had each other's backs for too long to just let some judge divide them.

Neglect had been the verdict. *Child endangerment.* Such senseless words considering how much care they lived by. Their mom worked nights at The Lunch Box, so Katy made sure her brother took a bath before tucking him in. And each morning, after Mom had a few more drinks and sank into bed to sleep it off, her brother made sure Katy ate breakfast before she drove him to school. Because though she was only thirteen, you didn't need a license to know how to drive, even if this was the very thing that got them caught. Pulled over for speeding in a school zone since Katy always had to be in a rush to make sure they were never late for anything.

They'd always been cautious, but one slip-up and everything breaks apart. A single misstep and kids end up in the custody of the state. They only live two towns away but haven't spoken to their mom in almost a year. So now all they want to do is go home. And tonight they have a strategy. Phase One: once they're off the grounds, they make their way to the nearest truck stop. Phase Two: call a cab. They have no money but figure when they get to the house they'll dig into their emergency fund—wads of ones stashed in a cookie jar on the counter.

The ride takes longer than expected, almost a full half-hour before the taxi pulls up to their address. All they can see through the darkness is the *For Sale by Foreclosure* sign, a bright yellow SOLD sticker plastered across the realtor's smiling face. They tell the cabbie to wait while they walk to the front door and turn the knob. Except they've been locked out. There was a spare key under the mat, but even this has been removed. They wait, unsure of what to do, until finally the porch light flares to life and the door opens to a man and woman standing in bathrobes.

"What the hell is going on?" the man says, his eyes creased against the glare of the bulb.

"Who are *you*?" Katy asks, putting an arm around her brother. She thinks she hears him sob, but soon realizes it's coming from inside the house—the wails of a baby waking up.

"We live here," the man says. "Who are *you*?"

The woman puts a hand on her husband's shoulder. "Can we help you two?"

Katy looks past them into the living room, which looks cleaner than before.

The smell of fresh paint lingers on the walls. Everything is new and rebuilt, and she wonders if they somehow arrived at the wrong house. This one feels too full to be their home.

The cabbie honks. The woman asks them again what they need. Katy's brother shakes his head and asks what they should do. Katy isn't sure what the next step is until the man says, "I'm calling the cops." And it's then she knows Phase Three, the only option left to them, as she takes her brother's hand and yells, "Run!"

And they do.

3.

Jill has rarely left her room since she arrived last Christmas. When boys on the other side of the dorm are caught smoking and then isolated in their rooms, they sometimes carry on for hours. Or when the new kid showed up a few days ago and had his knife confiscated, when he freaked out and had to be restrained, locked in the Control room until he calmed down—Jill just put in her earbuds and turned up the music. She doesn't understand why the boys hate being alone. It's all she ever wants. In fact, she's always been a Level One, none of her points taken, so she gets to have her music and Day Passes. But by law she isn't allowed back home, so Jill has never taken advantage of the all freedoms granted her.

There's a knock on the door as Penny walks in with a clipboard. "Room checks."

Jill is allowed to stay up until midnight with the light on, but considering the rash of escapees lately, the staff is cracking down.

"Did you get your homework done?"

Jill removes the earbuds and shrugs. Graduation is in a few

weeks, so she doesn't bother studying anymore. She keeps her room clean, makes her bed, vacuums the lounge after school. Similar chores she'd once had at home before her mother died. But now she only wants to follow The Program in order to prove up and leave.

Penny sits on the bed. "Your birthday is coming soon. Eighteen. Big year."

"I'm not staying," Jill says, knowing they can't do a thing after she ages out.

"You can, though. Three more years. Just to figure it out." Penny brushes back a shock of black hair from Jill's forehead. "Or I could call someone. Get you set up with an apartment?"

"My dad is waiting for me," Jill says, though she isn't sure it's true anymore. She hasn't spoken to him since she was taken by DHS after writing that damn poem. A social worker asked why she'd written it, how she was getting along with her dad, where she got the scars on her leg. She told them the assignment was just a metaphor. They were learning figurative language. That she got an A on the poem. But her homework became evidence anyway. In court, she told the judge that was the problem with poetry: it can mean anything you want it to. And without her testimony, the charges against her dad were dropped. But it didn't stop her from ending up here.

"Okay," Penny says. Except instead of leaving, the staffer turns around and lifts her own shirt, revealing the wounds along her back. "These were on the good days."

At first, they look like calluses, hardened instead of healed. But when Jill's fingers slide over the ridges in Penny's skin, the scars are soft to the touch, much like her own. "Good days?"

"When he was too drunk to do anything else," Penny says. "But even then he still had to find a way to take something. Some piece of me always belonged to him."

"That's messed up. But it's not the same."

Penny pulls her shirt back down. "How's it different?"

Jill wants to explain how her father never hurt her, ever.

That once her mother was in the ground, he spoiled her to no end. Let her skip school. Bought her new clothes, ice cream. That he'd do anything to make her smile. And eventually she didn't even have to clear the dishes or take out the trash to please him. Instead, she had only one chore, which was to make her father a little less lonely every now and then. She wants to tell Penny that it was something they shared. Something they both needed to make up for the loss in their home. Something nobody could understand. And what was wrong with a bit of comfort anyway, no matter what form it took?

"My father loves me. That's the difference."

"That's not love."

"What do you know about it? Locking kids up like inmates. Is that your version of love?"

"We do these things for your own good."

"Is that what your dad told *you*?"

When Penny tears up, Jill wants to say sorry. But she's tired of apologizing, tired of explaining herself, tired of being misinterpreted and punished for every word she says.

4.

Ryan is making a hypothesis. All things being equal, and with an agreed-upon premise of wormholes, time travel is not only a possibility but a probability. It's simply a matter of velocity. Velocity and mass. Mr. Johnson says by using the scientific method one could prove almost anything. That every problem has a solution. But it's their job to discover it.

So after school, once he boards the van with *Birmingham House* scrawled across the side, Ryan ignores the stares of all the other seventh-graders and thinks about the future. How his mom has six months left on her sentence. In her letters, she promises to stay clean. That once she's let loose, she'll come for him and take him home and things will be different from now on.

This morning Ryan discussed time machines with Mr.

Johnson, who said it would be a perfect experiment for the science fair. Theories were just as important as laws. Facts were facts. So during study hall, Ryan scoured the internet and was surprised to find so many clips of people, mostly old men in garages, who were well on their way. He took notes. Even sent a message to one of the scientists who said he'd already traveled back to ancient Greece, fought in the Trojan War, and was rewarded with a young handmaiden who died during childbirth.

But Ryan has no interest in the past. With his luck, he'd wind up in his own lifeline, meet his former self, and collapse the universe. Though it'd be an interesting test, wherein he could maybe warn previous-Ryan not to call 911. When he came home from school and saw his mother barely breathing on the kitchen floor, he could tell that other Ryan to just pour himself a glass of milk, order a pizza. Maybe she would've woken up instead of the paramedics taking her away. He lies awake most nights wondering if he made a mistake.

Or he could travel back to when his mom met his father. That was the first mistake: falling for a man who pumped her full of meth and then vanished like a card up a magician's sleeve. Ryan could go back, take his mom by the hand, and lead her down a different timeline that included just him and her and a home full of—if not happiness, then the closest thing to it.

When the van pulls up to the dorm, a squat brick building in the middle of nowhere, Ryan runs to his room and works out all the scenarios, all the redos he could remedy, until he at last finds the flaw in his theory: the time-loop. In each situation the problem remains the same. Even with science on his side, he could never save her. Even if he could rewrite the past, each revision led to another disappearance—her dead on the floor or him never being born, which in the end were maybe, all things being equal, the two better solutions.

5.

They love their prison stories. Mike boosting a car. Tanner and his drugs. Then the new guy, Carl, who can't shut up about pulling a knife at school. Many of them have been placed here from different parts of the state, so it's hard to confirm anything. And though they all have a feeling things aren't exactly as they say, there's a quiet understanding to not question the lies. But then there are kids like Jake who never talk. Who, when prodded, refuse to confess their crimes. So when Jake never makes eye contact, when he prefers to stay in the lounge, planted on the couch rather than go outside during Rec, that's when you know someone had it really bad.

And that's when the gossip begins.

The first rumor is confirmed by Hannah, who overheard Jake's counselor talking to one of the staffers. How he'd been pimped out by his own mother. Fifty bucks a throw to help pay for pills. Five tricks a week. Some of the boys are virgins and think it's ridiculous that a guy can get locked up for getting laid. "Boys can't get raped," they tell the girls in the lounge.

The second rumor is that Jake's sick. Hepatitis. Maybe HIV. He *is* tiny, more a child than a teenager. And his face does look pale, as if nauseated. And there's no denying he seems tired all the time. So though they want to haze him, nobody gets too close.

But on the evening he's removed from the house, there's no point in calling them rumors. When they first hear about it, the boys wonder where he's going. Back home? Placed with a foster family? None of the options seem fair until they run into the Day Room and see Jake being carted out on a stretcher. His wrists are tightly bandaged and he's unconscious. Once he's loaded into the back of an ambulance and driven away, the staff stands around the couch in the lounge. Their arms are crossed and their foreheads creased. They're not sure what to do about all the blood. The stains in the fabric are dark, almost black. Everyone is wearing green rubber gloves and holding towels. But as they start to clean, Penny runs into the room, yelling for them to stop, to not touch anything. That they need to call specialists.

The boys feel bad for the kid, at least in part. Though another part of them wonders if it was for the best. It's the same part that feels exposed, as if the air in the house has become toxic with something they can't fight back against. Something they can't see or punch or even ignore anymore. That evening, whenever they walk past the couch covered in a tarp, they feel a sudden hollowness, like the void left behind after a hair has been plucked.

None of them can sleep. So that night, while smoking outside after curfew, when Tanner flicks his lighter and says it's time to purge the place, rid it of the bad juju hanging about, they all agree to convene in the lounge. Mike says to start with the cushions. They'd light the quickest. But it doesn't matter because when Tanner puts the flame to the fabric, the whole couch goes up like a tinderbox, a giant inferno that sets the room ablaze in light. The boys stand silent, stunned as the fire dances like some kind of ancient sacrifice, the whole building vulnerable and ready to burn until finally the ceiling spouts water, dousing everything back into darkness.

6.

Birmingham House smells like wet smoke and Gabbi can't sleep. Mostly it's the night sweats, her whole body like one giant nerve stripped of its skin. But the burnt stink in the air, the way it fills her lungs, doesn't help. It's only been a few days since she was sent here, but it's long enough for the shakes to set in. She told her parents it wasn't a problem. She wasn't an addict or anything. And she thought it was true—but three days later and her back has begun to ache. Her legs always tremble. And her mind moves slowly, as if stifled with cotton.

So when everyone circles up in the lounge for Group,

Gabbi is the first to volunteer.

"I think I need something."

The counselor says, "Oxy is a powerful drug. Does anyone here have advice for Gabbi?"

Everyone stares at the scorched carpet, a black smudge in the perfect shape of a sofa, until the kid in camo raises his hand. Gabbi hasn't been here long but already hates him. He talks nonstop. How his mom is a total dictator; how she doesn't deserve her husband's name. He forces his father into every conversation, some war hero who died but still manages to linger in every word the kid says.

The counselor doesn't call on him, waiting for anyone else to offer a suggestion, but the boy speaks anyway. "I say she deserves it. It's the price you pay."

Gabbi wants to tell him to go fuck himself but doesn't want to be dropped a level.

Instead, she imagines a therapist is like any other dealer. A little flattery, a bit of pleading, and she'll score her dose.

"I'm sick," she says, and the counselor nods. Gabbi can tell he likes this talk of disease. "But don't all patients deserve something for the pain? It'll only help me heal faster, right?"

The counselor sighs and writes something on his pad. "That's just swapping one drug for another. What you need is this." He points to the group. "You need support."

"But each kid here takes something. Every morning they stand in line to get their fix."

"It's not the same. And we're not talking about everyone else. We're talking about you."

"It's not fair. Everyone here is such a victim." Gabbi feels a wave of nausea when she points to the camo kid. "Daddy died and Mommy was mean to me." She points across the circle to Jill. "Mommy died and Daddy was mean to me." Gabbi sits on her shaky hands. "What about people with real problems? Medical issues?"

"We're all trying to heal," the man says. "One issue isn't

more important than the next."

"Don't you get it yet, asshole? Nobody gets better here. We all just keep burning our own couches."

Gabbi receives a level drop for swearing, which shuts down the conversation as they move on to the next kid, the next complaint, until finally the group is dismissed. They put their chairs back and head to the yard for Recreation. Camo kid holds the door open for her. But before Gabbi can walk outside, someone grabs her arm and pulls her down the hall.

Jill leads her to a bedroom and looks both ways before closing the door.

"What's your problem?" Gabbi asks as the girl walks to her mattress and lifts the sheet. She digs into a slit cut in the fabric, pulls out three pills, and places them in Gabbi's hand.

"What are they?"

The girl says something about anxiety, about cheeking them, about how they make her feel fuzzy. But Gabbi doesn't care. The chalky pills sit in her palm like little pearls: beautiful and rare. She doesn't say thank you, doesn't apologize. Instead of worthless words, Gabbi shows her gratitude by popping all three and chewing them like candy. Pure bitterness fills her mouth. Then she swallows and shuts her eyes, waiting for her body to feel as close as it can to clean.

7.

Hunter's mom lets him drive. It's supposed to be a sign of trust. Something they've both been working on. She drops the keys in his hand without a word. There are no hugs. His mom simply slides into the passenger seat and clicks her safety belt. Hunter is happy to see her, excited to go home for the weekend. He's been fantasizing about his Xbox, his own bed, his mom's cooking.

But when he starts the car, she tenses: on high alert before he even shifts into gear.

Hunter wants to believe it's because he's fifteen and has a

brand-new permit in his wallet.

He tries to tell himself this is the normal reaction of any parent who loves her only son.

"Maybe this is a bad idea," he says, trying to let her off the hook. It took a month to earn the Day Pass, but right now he just wants to turn off the car, walk back into the dorm, and continue to dream about home.

"No. You deserve it." She attempts a smile. "Just go slow."

He puts the car in gear and tries to remember the way back to his house. His mom can't stop staring at the speedometer. It feels like he's being graded. Like he's already done something wrong. Guilty before proven innocent.

But he does have something to prove. He knows this. Last night, in his one-on-one, the counselor told him that when things get out of control, when he feels heated up, to think of his mother's face that night. The panic in her eyes when he pushed her against the wall. The way she dropped and covered her head when he broke the plate against the sink. He can't remember why he did it. Something about a curfew maybe? Or the F he got in Chemistry? All Hunter knew was that he felt so small and had to gain size somehow. But now, white-knuckling the wheel and going five below the limit, he feels like a little boy pretending to play a game of grown-up.

"Do you think Dad will be around?" he asks. It's part of his Program. The first step in going home for good is to "take responsibility." His father moved out last year, wasn't even there that night, but it doesn't matter. Hunter has made everyone's life harder. And he needs to fix it.

"Haven't talked to him," she says. "I have no idea what he does, and I don't want to."

Hunter wants to say he's sorry. It feels cruel what's been done to her—every man in her life leaving. But when he takes his hand off the wheel, when he reaches out to her, she screams.

For a moment Hunter feels like he's never going to get back to where he once was. That he'll always be a monster in her eyes—those eyes that night, so full of fear.

It's the exact expression she makes now as she grabs the dashboard and tells him to stop.

Hunter turns and sees the crossing guard in the street, a walkway full of children.

He hits the brake with both feet, instinctively reaching across the seat to brace his mother's body. The same thing she'd done so many times to him as a child.

The car screeches to a halt before they reach the crosswalk. The guard gives him a scowl. The children walk across the road, never knowing how close they were to danger.

His arm still holds his mother in place. Her eyes are still scared. Hunter clenches his jaw, feeling the heat of disappointment fill his body. But as he pulls away, she grabs his hand back, hugs it to her chest, and starts to cry. He's been the cause of so many of these tears he's tempted to do a U-turn, head back in the direction he came from. Except when he hits the blinker and twists the wheel to turn around, his mom just shakes her head and says, "That's the wrong way, son."

8.

Hannah watches the boys play ball. Spring has arrived. School is almost out. So on Saturday afternoons during Rec, she sunbathes. The campus is quiet on weekends. Many kids earn Day Passes to go home until Sunday night. But this week, Hannah was caught outside with the boys after curfew. Before Birmingham House, she lived on her own for almost a year, so rules aren't her strong suit. And there are a lot of rules here, one being that guys and girls can only interact in common areas: the lounge, the kitchen, outside during sunlit hours—all under supervision.

She isn't even allowed to have a bikini, so instead she wears her shortest shorts and tank top. Hannah had a growth spurt last year and has become accustomed to the attention. In fact, it's what landed her here, caught behind the gas station showing herself off for tips. She needed more money, and after months of leering and catcalls, all those guys getting something for nothing, it seemed like she was getting ripped off. She finally had a form of currency, and it felt too powerful not to use it.

When the cops picked her up, it didn't take them long to discover she was only seventeen and living in a trailer by herself. Both parents gone—one on the road, the other in the dirt—and though she was almost eighteen and had, in all honesty, been taking care of herself most of her life, the judge still sent her away. To a Level Twelve facility of all places, which meant coed dorms. So why would Hannah want to live alone when she had the chance to be in a building with a dozen guys who had no real choice but her?

The other girls here aren't ugly so much as worn down: greasy hair, pasty faces. But Hannah still has that new-girl smell about her, a trace of the outside world. And since they all knew her story, she quickly became a rumor on everyone's lips: hated by the girls but practically worshipped by the boys. So the other night, when Tanner tapped at her window and asked her to join them, when she sat in the circle of wild-eyed guys and slipped up her shirt, Hannah almost felt like one of those goddesses she learned about in school. One of those chicks who sang so right they made men crash into rocks. Some boys massaged themselves. Some looked away. But others just smiled, like Tanner, who offered her a smoke in exchange for a feel. And though she usually never allowed touching, with options so limited here, it seemed like a fair trade. Until Penny found them and they were all dropped three levels.

So today it's just her and the guys. They pretend to play softball, but she can feel their looks between pitches. The only other women are the weekend staffer, napping in her chair, and Jill, sitting under a tree, reading like a good little girl. Jill's getting out in a few days, so she tends to stay to herself: following the rules and probably making plans. Hannah used to do that. Studied all the time, kept under the radar, made strong grades—thinking it'd get her somewhere. But being smart doesn't always mean you're better off. And doing the right thing rarely helps anyone. She wants to say this to Jill, to warn her, but figures the girl will learn it on her own soon enough. Plus, who is Hannah to offer advice? If there really are answers out there, nobody's going to find them in here.

But this afternoon, no one else is even noticing Jill, especially when Hannah hears the ping of the bat, followed by a "heads up."

The ball falls a few feet away. They want her to react, to stand and throw it back. But Hannah knows better. She waits for them to come to her, and it isn't long before their shadows block the sun. They surround her, mouths open like a bunch of brain-dead zombies.

She plucks the ball from the ground and shifts it between her hands. "Lose something?"

Tanner looks over his shoulder. The staffer is gone, maybe to the bathroom, and Hannah feels the mood turn. She actually prefers to sneak around. All risk is about getting caught— and she always has been. But now it feels like she's working without a net. Tanner nods to the guys, who hesitate at first and then fall upon her like a pack of wolves. Their fingers bite into her arms and ankles as Tanner strips off his shirt, saying, "Somebody's about to lose something."

Hannah wants to yell for help, but doesn't want to make what's coming even worse.

Except just as he starts to unzip, a voice screams for them to *back off*.

Tanner spins around to face Jill holding an aluminum bat, black hair covering half of her face. Hannah has never heard the girl say a word until now. And though part of her wants to say thank you, another part of her wants Jill to just go away. The last thing Hannah needs is to be saved by some uptight bitch protecting the poor helpless sluts of the world.

"This is none of your concern," Tanner says. When Hannah

hears her own thoughts coming out of this boy's mouth, she finally starts to struggle. But their grip is too tight.

"Actually, it is," Jill says. The bat shakes in her hands. She chokes up on the handle and holds it out in front of her like a sword. "Now, why don't you just let her go?"

"You don't want to do this," he says, moving toward Jill. "You'd never forgive yourself."

And it's then that Hannah sees the girl doesn't have it in her to fight. That Jill's the one in real trouble. That maybe it was time to do something that'd actually help someone around here.

"Mind your own damn business!" Hannah yells. And when she stops fighting the hold on her, when the hands leave her body, Hannah lifts her shirt and says, "Hey, I'm right here."

Tanner's eyes widen as he stumbles toward her.

But as she lies back, all Hannah can think is how even goddesses never get to be the god.

She shuts her eyes, takes a deep breath, and waits for that first rough touch of skin against skin. But it never comes. Instead, in the quiet of the afternoon, Hannah can only sense a collection of soft gasps followed by the quiet crack of steel against bone.

9.

Sunday night and the dorm is dark. Sometimes, while in bed, Jill will hear the small sound of weeping, a faint murmur of whispers. But tonight all is hushed. And Jill is about to drift off when she detects a sudden shadow enter the room, a body sliding under her sheets. At first she thinks it's part of the normal nightmare—bodies falling upon her, again and again— but then Jill feels the minty breath on her face. Sees that hair, high and tight.

He takes her hand and says not to worry. That she's safe. He's not going to hurt her.

It's nice, holding a boy's hand. Until he opens her palm

and places a knife in her grasp.

"What are you doing?" she asks. "You could get in real trouble for stealing this."

"I think you know a thing or two about trouble."

It's true. Since yesterday afternoon, when Tanner was taken away in an ambulance with a mild concussion, she's been dropped several levels. But levels don't matter anymore; she's leaving in less than a week.

"It's for protection," the boy says. "For next time."

She often wonders about "next time." If home will be different from now on. Or if everything will simply remain the same. She grips the knife tighter.

"And you can't steal what's already yours," he says. "I'm just taking back what's mine."

She takes in the smell of his body and guides the boy's hand down her belly, across her hip. Jill can feel his breath catch, but she keeps leading him under her sweatpants and down her leg. His fingertips are unbearably smooth against her skin until they hit one ridge, then another, the scars lined up on her thigh like chalk marks along a cell wall, her way of ticking off the time.

"Why?" he asks, but it's the wrong question.

She waits for something else, a gesture to show they suffer the same. But when he doesn't make a move, Jill understands there's nothing more to say. The boy doesn't have any wounds to share. So instead she reaches into his camo pants and takes hold of him, tightening her grip so she can almost feel the pulse beneath. And when he, at last, lets out a soft whimper, Jill can't help but push her lips into his, as if this alone could somehow heal what hurts.

10.

Penny tries to remember the success stories. Kids who actually graduate the Program. But even then she never knows what happens next. At least while they're here, under her care, there's a small comfort in knowing everyone's a bit safer, for the moment.

Except then there are days like today, watching the girl step into the rusted-out pickup.

There are no hugs. No tears as she slides next to the middle-aged man behind the wheel. Jill can't even look Penny in the eye, hiding behind that shock of black hair as they drive off.

At times, Penny wishes she could plant a chip in their bodies. Like animals released into the wild, she'd track them across the miles, the years. See how the story really ends. If nothing else, they'd at least leave with something to remind them someone out there is watching. Instead, they arrive as a name on a form and then depart as strangers, never to be seen again.

Except today, when the truck reaches the end of the road and turns out of sight, when Penny's about to go inside—to do room checks, fill out incident reports, maybe put in her two weeks—the white cargo van pulls up and out walks the familiar figure of a girl holding her younger brother's hand.

Penny can't help but smile and reach out her arms to the siblings, who look so tired, like little lost pets. "Welcome back, you two."

But the kids don't say a word. They don't run into her embrace. Instead, the boy and girl squeeze each other's hands a bit tighter and simply walk on by as if they don't see her at all.

MOMENTARY DARKNESS

Gloria hadn't planned on talking to anyone at the funeral, much less the boy's mother, until she heard the guns go off. The first shot startled everyone, as did the next. Gloria couldn't help but cradle her stomach, surprised that maternal instincts set in so quickly. By the third and last crack of the rifles, all the mourners in their winter coats sat calmly through the sound like it was a natural part of the ceremony. All except the mother of the boy, who clamped her eyes and trembled as if all twenty-one rounds were entering her skin instead of the sky. It felt like a cruel joke until two soldiers handed the woman a folded flag. They let her pick up a handful of dirt to throw at her son's casket and then escorted her to a car. And though Gloria was supposed to be in class right now, was supposed to watch the eclipse with her father in a few hours, when the priest asked everyone to join them for a small reception, she knew there was no going back home.

She slipped behind the wheel of her dad's old Buick and followed the procession of strangers down streets of a town she'd never seen, never even heard of, until last week when the e-mails came back online and she saw the name. *Martinez*. For a brief moment there was relief as her future slowly returned. In fact, she felt something close to joy when she read the report about an IED blowing another man to bits. For days, she wondered what would've been in store for her if it'd been Heath's name instead, which only made the sickness in her stomach worse.

For twelve weeks, she'd been able to keep it quiet, but now the nausea rarely left her. Soon she'd have to make a decision. But then that e-mail arrived, and somehow made every life suddenly feel fragile. Which was maybe why today she woke before the sun and drove three hours to watch a body be lowered into the ground; in hopes that it'd make her feel more prepared for the moment when it came, one way or another.

However, during the funeral, she felt nothing. And this inexplicable emptiness bothered her more than the thought of Heath in that casket. So, now, as Gloria pulled up to the Martinez home, hoping just to feel something, it only looked like an ordinary house: small and filled with family. A weak winter sun tried to shine, almost vulgar in its indifference. And Gloria could no longer stand it: the silence of the street, the cold clear sky, the absolute disregard of the day.

When she went up to the front door and found it unlocked, Gloria walked right in without invitation, only to be flooded with the sounds of a foreign language. By the time she graduated last spring, Gloria had taken two years of AP Spanish, but this didn't stop her from feeling lost in the floating words. She wasn't sure who was related to whom. Bodies hustled from room to room with steaming dishes. Somewhere, a radio blared Mexican music. Gloria didn't even know Iowa had a Spanish station, the crooning of the singer's voice like some throwback to a bygone era.

Then she felt a hand on her shoulder.

It was an old woman, small and dressed in black, her face lined with deep ridges.

She gave Gloria a glass of water, drops streaking its sides, then gestured to the kitchen.

"I'm sorry," Gloria said. "I shouldn't be here."

In fact, her father had already left a voice message about this afternoon. He was a professor at Northern Community College, so Gloria's absence had probably been noted. She never used to skip school, never gave her father a reason to worry. But lately all the rules she'd tried to live by had begun to turn on her. Now it seemed almost foolish to be loyal to such laws.

The old woman hadn't moved, her face steady as stone. Gloria wondered if she was deaf.

"I didn't know him," she said, a bit too loud. "But he sounded nice."

The grandmother gave a slight smile and led her to the stove where women hovered over giant pots. Gloria never cooked. She knew how to boil water for pasta, but for most of her life she either got take-out or made cold sandwiches for her father. Gloria was five when her mom disappeared, and at the time she didn't think to ask about it, figuring it was just something mothers eventually did. Most of her friends had single-parent homes, so when the time came and Gloria's mom sat her down and said she needed to leave Bridger—that the town, their house, the entire state of Iowa had become too quiet for her—it didn't seem strange. But when she never came back, Gloria at last asked her father where mothers went. That day, he took her by the hand and guided her outside. They sat in the front yard, where he drew ovals in the grass with his finger, and for the first time explained how different worlds have their own orbits.

The women in the kitchen looked at her from the corners of their eyes.

The grandmother pointed toward the sink and said, "Lávese."

Gloria washed her hands and was handed a knife. Another woman, maybe an aunt, handed her a tomato and made a karate chop in the air. The fruit was firm between Gloria's fingers until the first slice, when red juice spurted out and made her want to throw up again.

A girl, perhaps a cousin, scooped the slices and dropped them into a sizzling pan of rice.

"Bueno," the grandmother said, handing over a green pepper.

When Gloria's phone rang again, she excused herself to the next room, listening to his latest message. *"At three, the moon will be in prime position."* It was nice to hear her dad's voice, though they hadn't spoken in days. He never liked Heath, a boy who had no plans beyond high school and didn't know the first thing about physics or the future. So three months ago, when her boyfriend returned from Basic Training, only to inform her that he'd soon be joining his unit in Afghanistan, Gloria's dad couldn't hide his happiness. Maybe now his daughter could move on, go to college, be her own person. But when the pregnancy test turned positive, Gloria dropped out, moved back home, and enrolled at NCC, taking classes in a building right next to her dad's lab where he taught Physical Science to other kids who had no idea what to do with their lives.

In the years since her mother left, they'd only missed watching one eclipse together. In the Bible, a book that always made her fact-minded father shake his head, it said celestial events were God's miracles. So last fall, the night before Heath was officially deployed overseas, when they made love for the last time beneath a harvest moon, Gloria thought it might mean something bigger than the both of them. She lay under Heath in the park, the lunar sky bright with the color of blood, and prayed their life together would never end.

And, in a way, it did make a miracle—another life she wasn't sure what to do with now.

Maybe it was a test to prove herself, to show her faith wasn't fake. Like on her sixteenth birthday, when the only gift she asked for was a new name. She'd been given her mom's, passed down from generations. But every time someone called her that word, it only made her want to turn around, as if they were talking to some other woman standing over her shoulder. She refused to even say it aloud, until finally asking for a name that was hers and hers alone. Her dad drove her to the courthouse himself, trying to guess what he'd have to call her now: Cassiopeia, Ursa, Orion. Until, of course, she signed the form and handed it to the clerk. Gloria could almost hear the question circling his mind: how could *his* child believe in the wrong kind of mythology?

Now, Gloria wondered if she'd been a fraud all along, trading one name for another like it'd somehow solve the problem of the past. Perhaps the whole "good daughter" act had just been a mask for her truer nature, which seemed hell-bent on betrayal. A trait forever born in the blood. Still, oddly enough, when the e-mail system shut down last week, all Gloria wanted was to talk to her dad, the one man who knew something about sudden losses. Instead, she sat in her room and stared at an empty inbox, waiting for a reply from around the world that never seemed to come.

In the living room, she deleted her father's voice message and was about to grab her coat when she heard the weeping. It was hard to detect above the rattle in the kitchen, but eventually she was able to trace the sobs down a hallway. The bedroom door was scuffed and timeworn. Along the frame were lines measuring height and age. It stopped at seventeen, the pencil mark almost as tall as her. But the last year remained uncharted, which was maybe why Gloria was really here: to fill in those gaps.

She knocked and the crying ceased, as if the small taps had scared off the grief. Gloria felt suddenly selfish, invasive. She wanted to slink away, hoping to make it in time for the eclipse—perhaps to share this with her dad was the only comfort she was capable of giving today—until the door gently clicked open. When the mom's face appeared, Gloria was shocked at the resemblance. Photos had been strewn about the funeral. He was handsome, despite the big ears and crooked teeth. But what was beautiful about him had obviously been inherited from her.

"Qué quiere?" the voice cracked.

"I just wanted to say..." But Gloria had no clue what to say. Thank you? Sorry? I'm glad it was your boy instead of mine? "I just thought you should know your son meant a lot to me."

The mother took Gloria's hand. "You know mi hijo?"

There was a slam of an oven, bowls being placed on tables, women whispering as if to make up for all the noise. They'd left the funeral an hour ago, but a strange kind of quiet had seemed to follow them here. And Gloria knew it'd probably never leave this house—these little whispers forever upsetting the silence. The mother looked confused, leading Gloria to the bed. It was tiny, a twin-size, only big enough for one body to sleep. The folded flag lay on the pillow, its tight creases sagging toward the center, a damp spot sitting in the depression of the cloth.

"De la escuela?" the mother said.

"No." Gloria sat down, sinking into the soft mattress. "We didn't go to school together."

"He was mal estudiante." The woman smiled at some far-away memory. Maybe her son getting detention, skipping classes. "Tímido. No amigos."

Gloria gripped the mother's hand tighter. "The guys in his unit. They knew him. They're all brothers over there."

"The Army no es familia." The mother sneered as if she was about to spit on the ground. "But no have otra remedio."

Gloria squinted at the last sound. "Remedio?"

"No have otra..." She looked above her, as if searching for the word. "Opciones."

Gloria gazed at the giant crucifix above the bed, the body of Christ slumping forward, eyes cast to the sky. "I've had some experience with that."

The mother's face lit up. "Y tu? Un soldado?"

"No, no. Mi novio. He's a soldier."

The woman's face went slack as she stared out the bedroom window. "Su novio," she sighed. "Afghanistan?"

"Sí," Gloria said, holding her belly with both hands. "Es un padre."

And though she thought the news would come as a gift, something that'd make any mother smile, the woman covered her face instead. Gloria wasn't sure if she misspoke—if maybe the one secret she'd kept from everyone had somehow been lost in translation. But when the mother started to sob, the tears coming on fast, Gloria saw that everything had been all too clear.

Soon, the woman sat up straight and brushed at her eyes. "Lo siento."

"Don't be." Gloria put an arm around her shoulders. "A mother who loses a child is supposed to feel this way."

"No." She shook her head and gently touched Gloria's stomach. "Lo siento."

The woman quickly stood, placing the folded flag on a nearby dresser, next to her son's senior photo. She straightened the dusty frame, smoothed her dress. Then she took a deep breath, whispered a quick "Me tengo que ir," and disappeared out the door.

At first, Gloria figured the woman simply had had enough goodbyes for one day, though the way she ran from the room felt a lot more like an escape. Maybe a pregnant girl at a funeral was bad luck. But Gloria didn't want to stick around to find out as she walked out of the house, got in her Buick, and broke the speed limit the whole way home.

In the front yard, her father lay belly-down in the snow, and Gloria assumed the worst until she saw the box in his hands. Buried in a thick coat, her dad looked so much older than she remembered from a few days ago. She slid next to him and wondered if she looked older as well.

"Last one for a while," he said without looking at her. "Maybe our last one together."

"Don't say that, Dad."

"By the next time, you'll have a degree. The next after

that, maybe a husband." His breath formed white clouds as he spoke. "A few more, you'll be watching with your own kid."

She didn't know why he was talking like this since the moon was already impeding on the daylight. By now he should've been explaining the differences between solar and lunar eclipses and why they're important in the universal precision of all the things she couldn't quite grasp.

Unless, maybe, her dad wasn't as oblivious as she thought. If perhaps he knew more to the story than he let on.

"Sounds like you've got it all planned out." She picked up the pin-hole box lying next to her father's shoulder. "But I don't know if I even want kids."

He sighed and lay back in the snow, slipping on his solar glasses. "You know, at these rare moments, two paths simply coincide. But in many ancient cultures, they saw it as an omen. The sun was sick or angry. So it abandoned them. Or the moon was a jealous lover trying to hide his beloved's beauty from us. Either way, most assumed it was the gods punishing them. But then, soon enough, we saw it for what it was—just an illusion. It doesn't mean anything."

"That's depressing."

"No, it isn't. That's where the wonder lies. Do you understand?"

And though it made little sense, she nodded anyway, knowing that to look toward the heavens for answers only brought out more impossible questions.

She felt his hand on her face, wiping the tears Gloria didn't even know she'd let slip.

"You'll be a great mother. Someday." He handed her his glasses. "When you're ready."

As the edges of the sun darkened, Gloria thought of the moon and how cold it must be. How for one moment during the day it looked like it was on fire. But her father was right, as usual. Despite how many times the two passed each other in the dark, they never actually touched—their merging simply a trick of the light.

Her dad clasped his hands behind his head, smiling like this might just be the end of the world. And, at first, Gloria was grateful for the quiet. But as the sun slowly left the sky, the sudden loss of light felt unfair. The world forced into a momentary darkness—a daytime theft that seemed both brutal and inevitable.

Gloria curled up next to her father's body, feeling his warmth as she stared at his strange smirk. "I don't know what's happening, Dad."

"Well, you see, the orbits run on an ellipse..."

Her father's words floated off his tongue like an old benediction he'd rehearsed for years, his face never ceasing to beam with a burning recognition of how things were supposed to work.

DOWN THE LINE

The day seems short, first break already come and gone. So though it feels like a quick day and the clock is running fast, my shoulders still ache. The joints didn't act up until last year, but now it's all they ever do. At night, I can barely lift my hands, as if it's a kind of permanent condition.

Right before Christmas, Ken Johnson, our newest foreman, told me I was getting behind.

I just smiled in return, saying, "Yes, sir."

Then he slapped me on the back, gripped a shoulder. "Get your head in the game, Jack."

But at day's end, as everyone left with their uniforms soaked through, Ken took me aside and asked if it would be best to quit while I was ahead. I said I'd do better until Ken mentioned the buyout—and I knew it wasn't about what I needed. He came around his desk, held out his hand, and said, "I have to admit, Mr. Dunbar—you had good run, old man."

Old man. It's what they call me. And not just because I've been here forever. Maybe a little too long since all I'm allowed to do lately is push a broom around, waiting out retirement.

Though now that it's come to an end, I fear the nickname is close to the truth. Today, as I sit in the cafeteria, my muscles are so swollen from all these years that the sandwich trembles in my hands. Carl and the others will be here soon, so I take this time to feel old before they remind me about it. I let my arms hang at my sides and take one last look around, this moment of the day when everyone isn't at work but instead far away from the sounds of machines.

But just as I start to think about what it'll be like on Monday when I don't hear the clatter of trays and dirty jokes, the boys arrive, loud and already laughing.

"Hey, Jack. Last day," Mitch Yates says. "How's it feel?"

"Different," I say. "Different but the same."

"What will you do with yourself now?"

"I'll stay busy." They nod their heads, but all I'm really thinking about is sitting in that kitchen with Greta. Reading newspapers, drinking coffee, and wondering what she's going to do with me around. If it'll be like when we first moved into the house, a sort of second honeymoon. Or if I'll just be something in the way. These are the things I think. How today feels like the end of something but, at the same time, the start of another something I can't quite figure.

"What you doing after work? Celebrating?" Mitch asks.

I shrug, say maybe. Carl peers at me from the corner of his eye because I already know about the surprise party. At his girlfriend's baby shower, Carl invited us out to dinner for my last day. I felt in his voice there was more to it. And it didn't take much for him to spill the secret.

"Place won't be the same," Mitch says, popping chips into his mouth.

I give him a wink. "Just discontinuing another line."

As they start in about making my press a tourist attraction, I notice Carl acting quiet. My grandson's usually the first to mouth off, just like his dad. But today he sits as if avoiding me.

"Carl," I say. "Will you please keep it down?"

He cuts me a look, his lips lifting into a smirk. "I'm just thinking."

"About what?" I honestly never know what's going on in that mind of his.

"About you," Carl says. "Leaving."

The boys nod like he's said something wise, but all I hear is a bunch of words.

In fact, for three years, ever since I got Carl the job, we've simply tolerated each other. I even trained him on the press myself, until he finally said, *"Okay, Grandpa. It's not like it's hard."* And there's a certain truth to this. Used to be a two-man job: one stamped, one stacked. But now the die drops the mold into the press with a simple push of a button. Then, for two decades, I've watched the hydraulics move with who knows how many tons of pressure until out pops another tire. After that, it's just a matter of watching it move on down the line for final inspection.

I wonder how many I've made over the years. How many kids like Carl have come and gone while I've remained, measuring time in reams of rubber.

Break is almost over when Kim walks toward our table to tell me good luck.

Everyone perks up. She started on the line a year ago and seems to be on everyone's mind though no one says her name. Today, she bends to give me a hug because I've always been good to her. I imagine how I look to a girl so young: a grandfather—the one thing you can trust.

Nobody looks her in the eye. She scoffs and shakes her head.

"Good talk, fellas," Kim says, sauntering off to a nearby table, but not before playfully tousling Carl's hair as she passes by. "I'll see you all tonight."

My grandson can't stop grinning. The boys eat in silence. And I don't talk either, waiting for the clock to tell me when to get back to it, one last time.

***

After work, we stand near our pickups and pass around a six-pack, sipping and not saying much. These last winter days in Iowa are short but severe, passing so quickly from one morning to the next it's like they hadn't been there at all. And though the wind slices through us, we sit in truck beds as if it's the middle of summer. Everyone takes their time drinking. I'm almost done with my second when I say I'm taking off. "Greta's probably worried."

They all nod again and say we should do something this weekend. That they'll give me a call—go bowling, watch the Hawkeye game. But they never look up from their beer cans, and I'd like to think it's just because they're still trying to pretend the party is a surprise.

I slip into my cab and look at the factory looming in the dim light. Maybe it's the weather making it seem so small today. When I pulled up to this building twenty-five years ago, it felt untouchable. But now I can't help but notice everything drooping. All the windows look half-cracked. Smokestacks blow white clouds of grit into the air.

Finally, I turn the ignition and throw her into first when Carl taps on my window.

"Remember, tonight at seven." I can smell the beer on his breath, the slur in his voice.

I say I know. To not worry about me. "And slow down on those, will ya?"

He slits his eyes at me. "You're not my dad."

"Boy, ain't that the truth." And I drive off without letting him get in another word.

Greta wasn't sure about taking in a grandson we'd never met. And there were plenty of rumors, as if he'd already become a duplicate of his daddy. Our own son had his share of trouble. Fights and detention. Even on the football field, he earned more flags than sacks. But when he joined the Army, for a second it felt like we'd done something right—until he came home and found the *For Sale* sign. I'd wanted to sell the farm for a while, so when developers came a-calling, and the factory opened up, we moved into Dexton and bought a house. But our boy refused to leave our land, taking on all that debt to resurrect the family plot. I couldn't help him, but I was hoping for him. He got a crop in the ground and a local girl pregnant, planting his seed any way he could. Still, soon enough, the final foreclosure came. But when the bank took possession, all they found was an empty barn and a body, the bullet still lodged in his brain.

Nobody ever talked about it, including Greta and me, until one day Carl called saying he needed a place to stay. He'd been in a group home but was about to turn eighteen—and his mom wanted nothing to do with him, which suited Carl just fine. Of course, it felt wrong for a parent to give up on a son, but who were we to talk about such things? So, in the end, it wasn't much of a choice—offering him a home and a job—even if we were too old to be raising another kid.

Still, bringing him into our lives also felt kind of fitting, like fate had brought back our son. Like last week when we went to their new house in Bridger for the baby shower—while Sadie opened gifts in the kitchen and the men smoked outside—it was as if my own boy spoke from the grave when Carl said, "She doesn't give it up anymore. How does she expect a ring when that's the only reason we're together?"

The guys laughed. But it was also like time-traveling back two decades. For a moment, I almost felt young again. And just as terrified. So when Carl offered up a little grin, as if awaiting my approval, part of me wanted to pat him on the back. While another wanted to slap some sense into him. Instead, I simply replied, "Be patient, son."

Then Carl got a real dangerous kind of quiet. "Shit, Jack, I hear enough of that at home."

Words like these make me wonder how much sorrow Sadie

hides behind that baby. Just a few months ago she called to say Carl hadn't picked her up from work. So I drove to the diner where she served me a slice of pie. I pushed the plate toward her instead, and Sadie ate like she hadn't done so in days. With no makeup on her paper-white skin, that bright orange hair pulled back tight, the girl looked about to fall asleep on her feet. And when she told me about the test turning positive, how she was unsure of bringing a child into a home about to fall apart, I didn't tell her one way or another. Still, she was looking for answers, so I repeated the same thing folks told me: "Do what feels right." Sadie said it helped though I didn't see how. Then she gave me a hug, her wet lips warm on my cheek, and made me swear to not say a word. She hadn't decided yet. So it was just something silent we held between us. Even later that night, when Greta asked about it, I kept my promise with a silly hope that it'd make some kind of difference.

Today, as I leave the factory, my heart races with so many of these ideas it feels as if there should be a banner to drive through, a parade I could follow. Instead, I pull away like any other day and wonder if it's true. If the guys will call me up to have a beer or if that's all over as well.

It doesn't take as long as I'd like to get home. But my house looks warm from the garage. So once inside, with my clothes stinking like a living thing, I undress right there in our kitchen.

Greta keeps her eyes on the sink of dirty dishes when she asks, "How was your day?"

I put a finger to my lips and walk behind her. She bends back and grins against my face, her breath becoming full-bodied. "Been drinking?"

Her skin holds the scent of shampoo, but sweeter than that. The smell of clean. I kiss her hair since it's always been the part of her that's never changed. She still wears her hair long, slick and dark, peppered with little grains of gray. It reminds me of a night sky, showered with stars that I want to taste and swallow. But I don't tell her any of this, assuming she knows it by the way I untie the apron and tug at her blouse.

We're late to dinner. The clock says it's time to leave, but both of us stay in bed.

Greta pulls the covers to her chin and asks what's the matter, but I don't have an answer.

Ever since Carl moved out and we've had time to ourselves, I haven't gotten it done. And today's no different. Of course, I know Greta's concern, as if it might have something to do with her, but the truth is I want to make love to her so bad I fear I'll burst. Though none of this helps.

It's finally decided to rain. I hear it strike against the windows, icing up the glass.

"It's okay, you know," she says.

"It's not." I sit on the side of the bed, my back to her. "Why would you say that?"

"You're just tired is all."

"That's not the problem."

"Okay." I hear the smile in her voice. An amused smirk she gets when I'm being childish.

"Why do you keep saying it's okay?"

"Jack, you're a good man," she tells me, as if this also has something to do with it. Her hands are on my shoulders, gently rubbing. "Don't do this to yourself. Not today."

"Seems as good a day as any." Maybe I'm trying to start a fight, but Greta won't go for it. Instead she stops massaging, as if her hands have grown tired. Neither of us moves. The tick of the clock gets closer to seven, but we just sit there, listening to each other breathe in the dark.

***

The surprise is a success. When we walk into the darkened Elk's Club over a half-hour late, the lights flip on and people suddenly appear from behind everything. We sit with Carl and Sadie. The Johnsons are there as well. Ken shakes my hand and introduces the brunette at his side—my foreman is twenty years my junior, but both he and his wife already look worn out from this life.

All the men have on their wedding-and-funeral suits. Carl doesn't say much. Takes two bites and is full. Sadie scrapes his leftovers onto her plate, slowly, in order to look less hungry.

But Carl glares at the pile of food, making it easy to sense the liquor on him.

"So, Jack," Ken says. "What now with you?" He wears a big grin like this is his way of saying good luck. When I say I'm not sure, he tells me, "Well, got lots of time to figure it out."

"True." Except it also feels like I should have some things already figured. It's not a time to be starting over. In fact, sometimes all that emptiness before me seems so endless it makes me sick. But when Greta puts her hand atop mine, I just smile and say it again: "That's true, Ken."

Carl stands and taps his glass with a spoon. Everyone watches my grandson's face turn pale, like he's forgotten what to say. It's not like him to get shy, but it may just be the booze. Or maybe it's something else. Either way, he has to close his eyes before saying it's time for a toast.

His voice wavers like the words are scratching his teeth.

Sadie shifts in her seat and looks at her plate, her long red hair falling in front of her face like a curtain. She moves a kernel of corn back and forth with her fork as if playing ice hockey.

"To Jack." Carl clears his throat and takes a sip.

People's glasses are still raised, their arms not sure what to do.

Ken Johnson hollers, "To Jack."

All the guests repeat the words and begin to drink when Carl blurts out, "No!"

"Carl," Sadie says, laying a hand on the back of his blazer. "Sit down."

"I'm not done yet." He turns to me, his eyes darting here then there, so wet I can't tell what's behind them. "Jack. Been around so long, hard to believe you're finally gone."

Some people softly laugh, but most don't make a sound until Carl takes a long drink and sits back down. Sadie rests her face in her hands.

I can't bear to look at her when a voice cries out from the back of the room: "To Jack!"

Everyone looks over their shoulder to see Kim standing in a black dress, glass raised.

The crowd repeats her words and drinks. Then talk begins again, as if nothing happened.

Greta grips my hand and tilts her head toward our grandson.

"That was quite a toast, Carl," I say.

"Toasts are a hard thing," Ken says, chomping away at his free food.

Carl kneads his eyes, as if chasing away an ache. "I think I need another one."

When Sadie pulls at his coat again, Carl bites his lip as if trying not to say something. But he does anyway. "Why you doing this to me?"

"C'mon, now," Ken says, using his boss voice: deep and full of bass. "Let's have some fun here." Then he goes back to his meal, figuring the matter closed.

"Stop it." Sadie gestures to her belly. "You promised you'd be able to drive us home."

Carl just stares at the empty tumbler in his hand, knuckles so white I know the glass will shatter soon enough. As if it's no longer about the baby or the booze or who's right about what.

It doesn't take long before he mumbles something under his breath.

Sadie jumps out of her chair, swift and sudden. "What did you say?"

My grandson looks at me, dead-on like a dare. "Just because you're going to be a mother, doesn't mean you're mine."

I grab Carl's arm, saying we need some air. But Sadie has already picked up Greta's glass. People look to our table, expecting another toast.

"And just because you're going to be a father doesn't mean you're any kind of man yet."

When she slops the wine in his face, Carl just sits there and smiles some more.

Sadie wanders off through the maze of tables. Everyone stares at their plates. Ken hasn't stopped eating. Greta has her hand to her mouth, unsure whether to laugh or cry. But when she starts to stand, I signal her back down as if there's no problem here I can't handle myself.

Carl puts his head under the faucet. His shirt's spotted red. The lights are so bright I have to squint. It's nicer than the bathrooms in the factory, the ones I polish daily. Still, the air has that same old scent: bleach and urine. I hand Carl a towel, but he pushes it away and says, "What a bitch."

"It's a touchy time, son. You can't be saying things like that to a pregnant woman."

Actually, Sadie's become more beautiful since she's been expecting. She'd always seemed not only young but under-sized somehow. I couldn't imagine her having the strength to be a parent. But now with the fat filling out her face she seems sturdier, less like a brittle thing.

"It's too much." Carl hunches over the sink to wash his hands. "I mean, it's not enough."

I'm not sure what he's getting at. When Greta had our son,

there was cause for worry, of course. But Carl's words sound more like excuses than reasons. "More tough times to come."

Carl clenches his eyes. "What am I gonna do?"

"You're going to be a dad. It gets better. Down the line."

"You gotta stop saying those things, Jack." Carl chuckles. "You sound like Aunt Greta."

"Why you acting this way? It's not right."

"Grandpa Jack. Always doing what's right."

When he looks into the bathroom mirror, I see my own stooped reflection behind him, like a shadow in the glass. I quickly straighten up. "Why are you always carrying on?"

"We can't all be so perfect."

If there's anything to laugh about, it's this. A man fired for getting old. A grandpa who can't get it up. I lean against a wall. It's cool on my bald spot. "I know what it's like, son."

"Stop calling me that." He paces the room, face dyed purple. His shoes tap the tile, making little clicks like gunfire. "Living under the same roof doesn't make someone your son."

I see his tears and think back on the last time I cried. Maybe my boy's funeral. Maybe not even then. "Okay, Carl. Have it your way. But I was the only father you ever had."

"Only because you had no other choice."

The light gives me a headache. The air moist with our breath. It's like I can't say what needs to be said. As if nothing's sinking in right. "I didn't have to take you into my house."

"Yes, you did." Carl crosses his arms like he knows some secret. "I was the do-over."

"The what?"

"For fucking up your own son."

My heart pumps so fiercely it hurts. My eyes are full of spots, like I'm going blind. All I can see is Carl standing there with his daddy's big grin, and it makes me wonder how much has been passed down. How much we may all be alike in so many different ways. But I don't want to just stand around thinking about things. All this talk makes me short of breath.

So instead I give my grandson a sharp slap across the face. The sound travels around the room like hands clapping.

"Now, you go back in there and apologize."

His body is a bundle of nerves ready to pounce. And though I'm ready for him to fight back, Carl doesn't do a damn thing. Just rubs his cheek, looking like he's real sorry for me.

I step forward and lift my hand again though I know I won't use it.

Carl laughs. "Jack, don't go trying to be something you're not."

Then the only thing I hear is footsteps, echoing, as if he's already far away from here.

I think about chasing after him, making the kid stand up for himself. But when I can finally move, all that's left is an empty room, the door softly closing in on me with a tiny hiss.

Outside the bathroom, Greta is waiting for me. "What'd he do? He hurt you?"

My vision blurs again. I can barely even feel the water sitting in my eyes. Greta takes my arm, leads me to a chair. The tables have been moved, guests jumping to music now, doing some kind of dance where everybody knows the same steps. "I'll talk to him later."

"Don't bother," she says, swiping at my eyes. "You shouldn't have even gone in there."

I have a hard time taking it all in with the music and the sting still sitting in my hand.

Greta gives me another of her smiles. "This is *your* day."

I watch the dancers, guys I've known for years grabbing women around their middles. Ken and his wife look on from the side of the room. I search for Sadie, for Kim, if only to tell them to stop putting up with these boys—that they're not even worth the trouble.

But, of course, by now, there's no sight of Kim. Only Sadie, slowly emerging from the crowd, big and beautiful. Greta asks her to keep an eye on me while she grabs a glass of water.

"She loves taking care of you," Sadie says, resting her arms on the bulge of her belly.

I stand, feeling my knees creak. "I don't need taking care of."

"Neither does your grandson, I suppose."

I gently put my arm around her, asking, "Do you need a ride home, honey?"

And when she gazes up with those wet eyes, I know she needs all the help she can get.

The house is dark and empty-looking. Sadie didn't say a word during the entire ride, but now can't stop the sobs. We sit there for what seems forever. The truck rumbles, rocking me to sleep.

"It's okay, dear," I finally say, though I can't see why this would make sense anymore.

"Are you sure Carl didn't say anything? I mean, to just leave like that?"

"He'll be back. We all do it sometimes."

"Do what?"

"Every man gets skittish about settling down. We just need time to make sense of it."

She nods. "Thanks for everything."

"Don't worry. I needed to get out of there as well."

"No. I mean everything."

I look down as she speaks and glimpse a naked thigh peeking through the slit in her dress. It's thick and pale, a brilliant glow right there in my truck, like a full moon to make a wish upon.

"Jack. Are you okay?"

I wonder if she noticed my stare, if she knew how lovely she is when bared to the light.

"It's a shame Carl doesn't appreciate you."

"You really are a good man, Jack."

I grunt again. "That's what people say, isn't it?"

"Just wish it'd rub off on your grandson. Sometimes I'm real jealous of Greta."

I want to know what there is to be jealous of exactly, but it seems wrong to ask somebody for that kind of thing. So I'm about to simply say thanks and goodnight when Sadie suddenly clasps her stomach, sucks in her breath.

"Give me your hand!" I offer it without thinking. She puts my palm on her. "Feel that?"

I shake my head.

"You missed it, I guess. He has strong legs." She smiles, her teeth white as well, but not as startling as her skin.

"Of course he's strong." I gently place my hand on her thigh. "Just like his mama."

I look up to see if she understands, but instead her eyes have grown big. Goosebumps quickly rise to the surface of her skin. And when she starts to shudder, I see she doesn't get it at all. That real strength is something the young will never know until they're no longer young.

And that I'm just an old man saying nothing new.

She brushes my hand away and says, "I have to go, Jack."

"I know you do."

"You should get some sleep," she says, giving me a sad grin. "You look tired."

"So do you, honey." Her face loses its smile so fast I'd give anything to take it back. As if I've said the wrong thing again—something too near the truth. "Don't worry. He'll return soon."

She tries another smile but can't quite make it a fact. And I don't blame her. But she leans over and kisses me on the cheek anyway.

Except as I watch her tail it up the driveway, it's like my lungs can't hold enough air. I put the car in gear, but before long it's so I can hardly steer, as if my heart won't bear another beat. And at first I think this is it. My days are finally done. But there's also something familiar about the feeling. When I pump my fist, slowly opening and closing my fingers, it's as if Sadie's right there in my palm. I touch it to my tongue and can almost taste the lingering tremble of her. Like maybe there's still a hint of heat, a little bit of fire left in these hands. The kiss stays warm on my face, making me drive faster, the blood burning up my veins so quickly I'd do anything to feel like my old self again, to make just one thing right tonight.

By the time I burst into the house, that empty hunger in the pit of my gut has only grown. So when I walk into the bedroom and see Greta taking off her earrings, I almost want to consume her. And though she starts in—"*Where were you, Jack? Had me so worried I made Ken drive*"—I don't let her finish. Instead, I pick her up until my shoulder tells me differently. I practically have to flop her on the bed before I start tearing away. Dress and nylons. Slip and bra.

She's under me, giggling, until I put a hand over her mouth and say to be quiet.

Her eyes, scared at first, give way as I enter her for the first time in so long.

And then I can't follow much of anything except the movement, the way she whispers "*Slow down*." But I don't, grasping the outline of her body, which is still firm for the most part but not all over, so that when it's done, I can't help but collapse onto the soft cloud of her skin. With my face pressed to the pillow, I focus on the rise and fall of her belly, our breath calm yet tense.

"What was that about?" she finally asks once our heart rates start to settle.

"I don't know."

She pets my hair, playing with my bald patch. "I wish you'd retire every day."

I put my head on her stomach, the slick skin so perfectly white it looks like it's sweating milk. Then I study my own skin dangling from its bones. The gray hairs matting my chest. Those old swollen shoulders. I snuggle close to her. "Did you like it?"

"Just surprised is all." She's still shivering, so I hold her tight.

"I hope I didn't hurt you."

"Jack," she whispers. "How could you ever hurt anyone?"

Then she smiles that smile again. I can feel it in the slight contraction of her muscle, sense its wave through the fullness of her stomach. The same place I laid my head after we made love for the first time all those years ago. The same place that once held our son, my small family starting from this one spot. So that now, as the night grows late, I put my ear to her body once again and listen closely for a tiny kick. Those little signs of life that may still remain.

VANISHING POINTS

The skies looked mean all morning. It'd rained earlier, so the heat had been cranking like a kiln since sunrise, making October feel more like midsummer. In fact, when Garrett pulled his Triumph up to the Dexton County Courthouse, the entire state was already under watches and warnings. His body felt blurry from the lack of sleep, but the ride had completely numbed his face. He never wore a helmet, even if Wendy said he was a father now and should be more cautious. But if Garrett learned anything from his own dad, it was that safety was never the point.

The courthouse was quiet today, and like every week for the past month, Garrett Miller signed in with reception, who led him to the bathroom, cup in hand. He left the UT by the sink and walked to Murphy's office for the Breathalyzer. When Garrett blew a zero, the PO leaned back and asked about the baby again. "Thing have a name yet?"

"You have suggestions, Murphy?"

"Yeah, Miller," he said. "Stay straight and get a job."

Murphy hadn't cared much for Garrett from the first, figuring him just another lost cause.

But he still set up two interviews a week to satisfy the

courts. Of course, no place wanted a nineteen-year-old ex-con handling their money. It was his first offense, but after posting bond, his mom couldn't afford the fine. So Garrett got ninety days instead of a deferment. Murphy said he was lucky. A few more ounces and it would've turned Possession into Intent. And though this may've been true, jail was still jail, even if he only served half his original six-month sentence.

"So work is hard to come by." Murphy opened a drawer. "But you can still go places."

"Are you telling me to break probation?" Garrett asked.

"There're ways to leave without leaving." He slid a brochure for Northern Community College across the desk. "Ever thought about learning a trade? They have several programs."

"How much does it pay?" Garrett said.

"Better than living on assistance. Start investing in yourself. Got others to think of now."

That morning, before Wendy woke up, Garrett stood over their daughter's crib. It amazed and terrified him that this person depended on him for everything. Each time her eyes fluttered, Garrett wondered what she dreamt about—if babies even dreamt at all.

"Plus," Murphy continued, "if you register as a student, no more job interviews."

"I think I'm better off with minimum wage."

"I've made an appointment at NCC for this afternoon. They'll get you in a few late-start classes. Don't show up, you're in violation." Murphy stood to signal they were done. "And name the damn kid already. Two months is too long. It's no good for her to not know who she is."

When he stepped into the trailer, Wendy was pacing the room, their baby screaming in her arms.

"I don't know what to do," she said. "I need some sleep and we're out of formula."

Garrett dropped his keys on the table, along with the application. "Should I call Mom?"

"Oh, wouldn't she just love that?"

"Let me try." Garrett took the baby in his hands, and soon quiet fell over the room. Until recently, she rarely cried. Even when she arrived three months premature, Garrett calling from the prison phone bank for updates, the child silently emerged into the world as if already knowing what little good complaining would do. For the entire month of August, she lay in the NICU, refusing to be named until they were sure she'd survive. And when the baby was strong enough to take home, Wendy promised to wait until Garrett got out—wanting to name her together. But now, it'd been a month, and they still weren't sure what to call anything anymore.

Wendy floated across the room like a deflated balloon. "How was the meeting?"

"Murphy wants me to register at NCC."

She laughed and rolled her eyes, suddenly looking her age. At times he forgot she was only seventeen. That they'd been forced to grow up fast, even if it was for different reasons. And though he was to blame for both, he also knew mistakes were a two-way street.

"What's so funny?"

"Nothing." She slumped down on the sofa. "Go to college. We'll just put it on our tab."

Her voice had only lately become bitter. Last February, on their first and only date, Wendy kept talking about how she wanted to go to every state, get any kind of distance from this place. It was clear she should've been the one planning campus tours, filling out applications.

"I guess it's better than just riding around all day," she added. "Right?"

"I got things I have to do. It's not like I get to just sit around the house."

"Is that what I'm doing?"

He sat close enough to smell the musk of her body, but didn't know what to say.

Maybe something about love, though they'd never said the word before.

In fact, for years they'd only seen each other in the halls of Roosevelt High, but never actually spoke—until last Valentine's when she asked him to the dance. His recent arrest had apparently boosted his reputation, and though Garrett wasn't much for school, after being bailed out by his mom, he felt obligated to go. Partly to prove something, but also because it felt close to normal—the idea of a dance sounding so pure and simple. They posed for photos and drank punch and by the end of the night, with no curfews and the car parked near a quiet pasture, it felt like there was only one thing left to do. All he can remember from that night was how they didn't look at each other, refused to touch afterward. Then he drove her home and they never talked again—until she missed her period. It was just a couple of months before jail when she called with the news: like another verdict coming down from a higher court, telling him what his future now looked like.

This afternoon, as the baby drifted off, he put his other arm around Wendy, tried to pull her close. But she shrugged him off the same way she did every night in bed—always making Garrett feel both relief and shame each time she pushed his body away from hers.

He stared at his child, the pacifier puckered in her mouth. "She looks just like you."

"I know," she said, still not opening her eyes.

"Maybe that should be her name, then. Wendy Miller. It has a nice sound to it."

"Oh," she yawned. "I think she deserves a little better than that, don't you?"

The clouds hovered like a hangover when Garrett pulled away

from the trailer. His mom lived in a double-wide down the row, and she'd never fully forgiven Garrett for leaving her. First, for prison. Then, for a new family. So, before serving his time, she co-signed on their trailer, saying it was a graduation gift but really just wanting to keep him close.

Yet today, as he rode past her place, he didn't stop, wanted to keep moving, but no matter how fast he went, the air was still suffocating—wet and heavy as the day, years ago, when his dad arrived with a Triumph in the bed of his truck. Bad coil assembly and dirty carburetor, but his dad said it was a steal, a word that made Garrett wary. The man had been in and out of jail his whole life, so Garrett hoped it wasn't an accessory to anything to say yes. Because, even if the thing looked half-ridden to its grave, he still held some childish fantasy about fixing it together, like all those dads and sons on TV. But the next day, he woke to find the truck gone, evaporated into the air like a mirage, leaving nothing behind but a broken-down bike as a goodbye.

Today, on his way to NCC, Garrett caught that first gust of wind, when the cold comes too quick and the sun gets stolen from the sky, like the clouds could split open at any second. He remembered how each time a twister touched down in their town, his dad would guide the family to the bathtub, insisting their trailer was strong enough to outlast any storm. And though Garrett knew the danger that lurked behind such delusion, today with the bike swerving between his legs, he had a desperate need to believe in anything, even if it was just a lot of wishful thinking.

The campus bustled with kids. After a half-hour of wandering, Garrett tried to ask for directions. But everyone at NCC walked with a mission, like they all had somewhere else to be. He wanted to call Murphy, say he was lost and running late, when he heard a voice ask, "Garrett Miller?"

That was the problem with small towns. Everyone knew each other. Had the goods on each other. And you couldn't escape no matter which way you turned. But he barely recognized the girl in front of him. Gloria Dempsey graduated a year before him, and though she'd always been small, today she was a skeleton of herself. Her yellow hair was shaved down on the side. And the eyes, dark and hollowed out, looked like they'd just seen someone raised from the dead.

"How's Wendy?" she asked, holding a notebook tight to her chest. "And that little one?"

"They're great."

"Wendy Jamison having your baby," Gloria said, shaking her head. "Hard to believe."

"What's that supposed to mean?"

"Nothing," she whispered, unable to look him in the eye. Instead, she stared off over his shoulder, her face suddenly looking sick when she asked, "What are you doing here?"

Before he could answer, her boyfriend had walked up on them, fists balled up tight.

"Hey, Heath," Garrett said, tired of people sneaking up on him today. "How you doing?"

He'd known Heath since grade school and had once considered him a friend. But since arriving stateside, Heath had become jumpy, which made it tough to figure out what he knew—how much Gloria had told him about the bonfire last winter.

"Came to give you a ride," Heath said, panting as if short on air.

Gloria shrugged and gave Garrett a nervous smile. "I'll talk to you later, okay?"

"He won't have time for that. Right, Garrett?" Heath puffed up his chest and grabbed his girlfriend's hand. "Don't you have some jailbait to knock up somewhere?"

But by the time Garrett could a say word otherwise, Heath was already dragging Gloria away. The campus had cleared, leaving behind a strange silence as he watched his old friend haul a bone-thin girl down the sidewalk. He tried to take a breath, get his mind right, but the air got trapped in his lungs, his body suddenly heavy. And though it was almost time for his appointment, Garrett had been taught a long time ago that when that cage came down around you, the back of a bike was sometimes your only way out.

When he walked into the dark trailer, a small burn caught in his chest.

Since the baby was born, Wendy hardly left home. So, though it'd be nice to be alone for once, anything that felt too good was probably bad—and a quiet house was never promising. He went from room to room, waiting for the baby to let out a little cry like a breadcrumb, until he finally found Wendy in bed, taking a nap. The baby was in her crib by the window. And upon seeing his family asleep, the exhaustion of the day gripped Garrett like a drug. He lay down and put an arm around Wendy, taking in the smell of her unwashed hair, until she gave him another of her half-hearted shoves. Still, he shut his eyes, and in that darkness, listened to his two girls: one dreaming of the distance it would take, the other maybe not dreaming anything at all.

Bonfires were usually small, a dozen kids at most. But last winter, on the day of the solar eclipse, a giant crowd from both Dexton and Bridger came out to celebrate the cosmic event. Really, it was just another excuse to start drinking at noon. So despite the cold, by the time the sun set, a party was in full swing. Some did a primal dance around the fire, like a sacrifice to the gods. Others wore moon-shaped sunglasses or stickers of stars on their cheeks. Everything felt on the brink of chaos by the time Garrett arrived, hoping to simply make a deal and get out of there.

At first, Garrett couldn't find his guy: another stuck-up Bridger kid who lived across the highway—but who also had dime bags for sale. For years, the county had debated on where to put Highway 20, a new four-lane that'd connect a string of towns. And Dexton had been on that path until a last-second vote called for zoning to go through Bridger alone, along with rumors of backroom deals and broken promises. So it wasn't long before farmers were forced to sell, Dexton diminishing as Bridger began to grow. Someday, they'd have their own school district, but until then the Bridger kids were stuck at Roosevelt High with the rest of the rubbish.

After ten minutes of walking around the party, he heard a low whistle from the woods.

At the edge of the field, a pale face glowed against the dark like some kind of lost ghost emerging from the snow. The boy gave another whistle, waving a baggie as if it were a dog treat.

"Okay, I get it," Garrett said, making his way into the drifts. "What you have for me?"

"Well, Miller," he said. "That all depends on what you're looking for."

"I was hoping for a little loan, maybe. I'm kind of strapped."

"There's no layaway here." He wrapped his fingers around Garrett's wrist, like a secret handshake, and placed an almost empty bag in his palm. "But there's just shake left. So, I want you to have it. There're always other ways to pay people back."

With the pressure of the boy's touch, the heat of his skin, Garrett felt dizzy, close to collapse. He had to jerk his hand away to escape the hold. "I'll get you back later then. Okay?"

As Garrett stuffed the bag into his jeans pocket, the guy smiled, saying he couldn't wait.

Next to the fire, Garrett had to take a seat, his mind gone fuzzy. He just wanted to go to his mom's and light up, sleep away his nerves, until Gloria staggered toward him and fell in his lap.

"Hey Gloria, I've never seen *you* at one of these things?"

"When the heavens align, expect the unexpected." She wore a coat and a pair of black goggles around her neck, which she held to her eyes and said, "Why, see something you like?"

Her breath reeked of whiskey, but beyond the slur in her voice, Garrett could also detect a want in her words. It'd only been a few months since Heath had been deployed, but here she was, already on the prowl and searching for a substitute. "Heard anything from your man?"

"E-mail was shut down for a while." Gloria dropped the goggles and laid her head on Garrett's shoulder, her long hair draping her face. "But I did go to a funeral today."

Beer cans cracked open. The fire snapped. Trucks circled the field, lighting the dark. Soon couples would head to those cabs, small squeals rising above the rumble of engines.

"Sorry to hear that. Anyone I know?"

She shook her head. "Nobody I knew. But does it matter? Kids you'll never meet die every day, taken from us without anybody else even knowing they were there in the first place."

Gloria sat up, her whole body shaking. At first, Garrett blamed the cold—until she touched her belly, rubbing it like she was about to cry. Or just throw up.

"You should go home."

"And I want to go anywhere else but." Then she smiled and slid her hand into his pant pocket. "So I figured you'd be holding something to take me to another world." Except when she touched the baggie, her fingers lingered, slowly massaging him instead. "Or maybe another life."

Perhaps it was a way to get back at Heath—for going overseas, leaving her behind. Or possibly she was just lonely and looking for someone simple to help her escape. Either way, she was struggling against something. And that night, Garrett just happened to be the answer for it—until she stopped herself with a sigh, as if ready for anything but the softness hidden in her hand.

"Seriously?" Gloria's body slumped over, like she'd been

suddenly emptied. Then she closed her eyes, her voice on the verge of tears as she whispered, "What's wrong with me?"

He wanted to ask her the same question, to know what his problem was, when out of the shadows came the shriek of sirens, followed by a red blaze of police lights filling up the night.

Thunder rattled the trailer, waking them with a start. As the boom faded, they waited for the baby's cry. But when it never came, Wendy had to place a finger to his lips to stifle the laugh.

"What time is it?" she said, her face inches away.

"Late, I think." The sky had clouded over, shedding a supernatural light across the room.

Garrett's eyes struggled to adjust, bringing a small ache to his temples.

He couldn't recall his dream, but a ghost of it remained, the erection still tight in his jeans. So far they'd been able to ignore the fact that neither had seen the other naked since that first night in his car. And as long as he focused on the baby, things made a certain kind of sense. But now, close to each other in bed, a hush fell upon them like an obligation. He put a hand on Wendy's leg and went in for a kiss, until she put a palm to his chest and said, "It's been awhile."

"Is that my fault?"

"Nobody's fault." She slipped out of bed and went to the crib. "It's too soon anyway."

"Actually, it's been eight months. And we have a kid together. It's not natural."

"Not natural," Wendy whispered, looking out the window. Lightning sparked in the distance. "You're right. And neither is going to jail."

"That's over." Garrett felt sweat surface on his brow. "I did my time while you got to live your life. And I never asked a thing from you."

"You're right. While I lived here alone and my water broke. And had to ask your mom for help. And be in the hospital for weeks. I never heard word from you. Not then, and not now."

Garrett stood next to her at the window. Dust lifted from their gravel road and swam across the yard. "You say it like I had some kind of choice."

"There's always a choice," she said, as if talking to herself.

"Maybe." Another dash of light streaked the sky. He counted the seconds until the rumble arrived, rattling the windowpane. He wondered how much it'd take for the glass to break; how much time they had before the downpour was upon them. "At least, it's a nice wish to think so."

When the thunder wouldn't stop, the baby finally began to stir. "She'll be hungry soon."

Garrett stared out at the green skyline. "I forgot the formula."

She bent to kiss her daughter's face, stroking that full head of hair. "Of course you did."

Outside his mom's trailer, he could see light flicker from the TV. The sun hadn't set, but the air felt electric. In the distance, a shadow of rain fell over the fields. It looked minutes away, but it was just the plains playing tricks. What felt so close was actually far, miles spanning between you and that vanishing point on the horizon where the world seemed to fall off and fade away.

His mom answered the door in her bathrobe, a menthol smoldering between her fingers. He rarely saw her wear anything else in the years since his dad left town.

"I need to borrow the car." He pointed to the black clouds above.

"Need to sell that damn thing. Bikes are for boys, not men. Get a minivan or something."

"The baby needs formula." He almost asked for some money

until she took a deep breath, as if gearing up for a lecture. But when he kept quiet, she could only sigh and wave him inside.

"The baby this, the baby that. Feels sinful not having a name."

"We've talked about this. We'll do it when the time is right."

She rummaged in her purse. "Seems like that time has come and gone."

Maybe she was right, but at least Garrett could still pass along his last name—the only other thing his father left behind. "You'll be the first to know, Mom."

The TV was muted, people on a game show silently shouting.

"You guys need to go to the courthouse. Get official. Stop making that baby a bastard."

"Don't talk that way."

"Not saying Wendy's my first choice either. Doesn't know the first thing about anything. But you made your bed, Garrett." She gripped the keys. Her eyes began to glisten. "Made mine too, I guess. Didn't stop me from raising you best I knew, though. Don't go proving me wrong."

Garrett held out his hand. "I'm doing my best too."

She gave him a kiss on the cheek, attempting a smile. "Lucky you still have me. Right?"

Once outside, Garret fired up the rusty Impala and shoved it into Drive, curious about how he and the baby would ever survive one mother, much less two at the same time.

The generics were sold out, so Garrett had to get the good stuff. Near the pharmacy sat a display of flowers floating in plastic pots. And though it'd be wise to buy Wendy a gift—a way to say sorry—the sight of all those pills behind the counter made him cringe. Not at the drugs, but at the counter itself. He didn't dream of being a pharmacist, but to know he could never be one now felt unfair. NCC probably had classes on how to read scripts, but he'd go forever not understanding what those words meant, making the idea of flowers seem silly.

Especially when the front clerk swiped his EBT card and the register beeped back. On the second failed attempt, Garrett told the cashier to try again, wishing he had actual cash in hand. After the third, when the clerk asked if he had other means, Garrett was tempted to walk away empty-handed until a voice behind him asked, "We have a problem here, Miller?"

As the ghost-pale face rose over his shoulder, Garrett wished he could disappear entirely, drive to some far-off place where no one knew his name. Except there was the baby. And Murphy watching his every move, and his mom setting her hopes on him, and Wendy waiting back home—and, of course, the boy next to him in line, whispering at his ear—so that running away felt like nothing but a dead end. Unless he wanted to look like he had something to hide.

"I guess," Garrett said, letting the guy take the formula from his hands.

"Looks like you owe me again," he said, sliding over a twenty. Then with a few taps, the register wound down to zero, every-thing bought and paid for as if it'd never happened at all.

They sat in the Impala, staring out the cracked windshield. The breeze had picked up again, blowing a stray cart across the parking lot.

"Going to get bad tonight," the boy said. "So, how's father-hood treating you?"

Garrett studied the formula in his hands. "When did you get back into town?"

"A couple days ago. Family stuff. I return to school on Monday."

Garrett never met anyone who went away to college. He pictured lecture halls filled with important ideas, kids reading under trees. All the things Wendy wanted but would never know.

"I'm applying to NCC."

"That's nice," he said, touching Garrett's shoulder. "And how's that girlfriend doing?"

"What do you want?"

He gave a low whistle and massaged his fingers into Garrett's neck. "Depends on what you're looking for, Miller."

Garrett felt flush, the breath stuck in his lungs again. "Actually, I could use a hook-up."

"I see." The boy raised a brow. "Sorry, Miller. I don't accept food stamps."

Garrett shrugged off his hand. "Even for people who don't snitch on their dealers."

"So you're saying I owe *you*." He clapped his hands, like he just got the punchline.

"I know how it works," Garrett said. "All the rich kids are allowed to go free. And guys like me go to jail."

"Is that what you know?" He grinned, his teeth dark against his pale face.

"I know enough."

"My mom's sick. You know that?" Garrett couldn't stop staring at that mouth, the way it kissed the air with each word. "She just sits around, smoking her prescription all day long."

"Well, we all have problems. Probably have a big inheritance coming your way now."

The wind stopped for a moment, the air dropping by a few degrees. In the distance, clouds lit up like lungs in an X-ray.

"Won't be long now," the boy said. "Can't believe you're a dad. What's the kid's name?"

"Okay," Garrett said. "I think we're even here."

"Nothing changes around this place," he said, struggling with the ancient seatbelt. "In fact, how you ever ended up with a baby is beyond me."

"Well, there you go. I guess some things do change."

"You think so, huh?"

Garrett was worn out with one-sided questions. This conversation needed to end. But as he reached over to open the passenger door, hoping the guy would take a hint, Garrett was instead met with a mouth that felt more like fire than flesh. It only lasted a second, but Garrett swore he felt a heartbeat between his lips. But then he felt the guy unzip him, holding Garrett hard in his hand, those same soft lips twisted into a smirk, as if they knew something he didn't.

"I bet you just *loved* it in prison, didn't you?"

Garrett had never punched anyone before, but it wasn't like he'd imagined: the way it hurt the fighter as much as the foe. As he rubbed the ache out of his knuckles, the boy simply stooped over, cradling his nose. But then the whimpers began. And all Garrett wanted to do was say sorry, ask how he could help, until it soon became clear the sobs were actually laughs.

"Well, I guess that proves it." The kid slipped out of the car, slamming the door behind. But not before he tossed a baggie into Garrett's lap and said, "You're a changed man."

The radio squawked about sightings of supercells, radar-indicated rotations, a possible tornado touching down. As Garrett sped down the road, he felt clouds swirl overhead. The wind knocked him between the lanes. The engine hammered like it'd come apart if pushed, and the last thing he needed was to be pulled over. Garrett could almost hear his mom's voice, talking about apples not falling far from their trees, as he rolled down the window and threw the baggie as hard as he could—though it was hard to tell if it'd ever be far enough.

He pulled up to the trailer and saw his bike on its side. Then the rain quit, as if sucked into the sky. Like all the wishful thinking in the world could no longer stop what was coming.

Inside, Wendy stood by the stove, the baby asleep in her arms. "Where were you?"

Garrett held up the formula. "I got it."

"My hero. What took you so damn long?" she yelled, causing the baby's eyes to jerk open. Garrett braced himself as his daughter's voice filled the room.

"Great," Wendy shouted to the bundle of blankets. "I can't handle this anymore."

"Stop it, Wendy." He took the baby from her. "You just scared her."

Wendy's eyes cut across the room and Garrett waited for her words, harsh and revealing.

Instead, her face softened. And when she lightly laid her hand on his, it almost felt like a pardon, until she asked, "What happened to your hand?"

He pulled away from her, the baby somehow feeling heavier in his grip. "I'm fine."

"Are you?" she asked, crossing her arms. "Because it sure looks broken to me."

He wasn't sure what to say—until the sirens wailed across town, their sound descending like a scream. Garrett shoved the little body back into Wendy's grasp and said, "Into the bath."

"Where are you going now?"

Outside, he had to stride against the wind and fight his mother's trailer door open. She was still on the couch, watching weathermen on TV.

"They haven't shut up about it," she said. "Now I'm going to miss my shows."

"It's happening, Mom. Why don't you come over to our place?"

Garrett expected a struggle, but instead her face filled with a joy he couldn't quite figure.

She took his hand as he led her to their trailer where they found Wendy in the bathroom, rocking the baby and shushing into her ear.

"You two get in the tub," he said.

His mother started to step in when Garrett stopped her. "I meant them."

Her face went slack as he helped Wendy into the stall.

Garrett listened for the baby, her cries hard to hear with the wind whipping at the walls.

"It'll all be over soon," he said, knowing that, unlike other threats, tornadoes came quick and left just as fast. You almost didn't see them until they were on top of you, taking up all the oxygen, filling your world with debris. Then before you knew it, it was gone, hitting your house but missing your neighbors' like some kind of lost traveler in the night.

"Just in case," Wendy yelled. "I want you to know. I named her after my mother."

"What are you talking about?"

"We couldn't leave without a name. To take her home she needed a birth certificate."

There was a sharp snap, and the room went black. Garrett blinked as the sight of his family disappeared into darkness. The only thing still alive in the room was his child's fragile sobs and the sound of the warning sirens with their steady ability to break everything open.

"Hello?" Wendy asked. "Garrett? Are you there?"

Garrett nodded, though he knew in the dark it did no good comforting her fears.

When the trailer shifted in the wind, he wondered if their little house could withstand the destructive desires of the oncoming storm or if they, too, would blow away for good.

"It's a nice thing to do for your mom," his mother said. "What's her name, honey?"

"Hannah." She took Garrett's bruised hand and shouted, "Her name is Hannah Jamison."

Garrett said the name aloud, then whispered in her ear: "I like the sound of that better."

Though thicker now, Wendy was still small enough to reach his arm around. He had no idea how someone so short had survived the growing heft inside. It was a miracle she hadn't been torn in two. So now, crammed so close in such a tight space, he gently touched her waist and waited for that faint but familiar nudge of her body away from his. But, instead, as another gust shook the house, Wendy pushed the baby into Garrett's hands and locked her arms around his neck, the inescapable weight of her embrace making it all but impossible to breathe.

LIMITED JURISDICTION

Amber alerts were everywhere tonight. DOT signs flashed statistics: height, weight, age. Earlier this evening, when Heath went over the precinct assignments, handing out digests for the shift, there among the usual files was Maria Diaz: a six-year-old who didn't come home from school.

The alerts informed people of her colors—hair, eye, skin—but they were really intended to strike fear into families. A missing girl. A white Camry. It often sparked enough panic to bring the missing back within a few hours. But at tonight's briefing, the real details emerged: a dad with no custody rights and extended family in Arizona. So they'd likely cross state lines, putting it out of Dexton's jurisdiction once again.

It was the same old story. Fathers always the first suspects.

Two hours on patrol—driving main drags, canvassing backroads, cruising foreclosed houses and other abandoneds—Heath had yet to receive a single call. In his twenty-five years on the force, even now as county sheriff, he couldn't remember a time when the streets felt so empty. Maybe it had something to do with the cold front: mid-January with its bouts of snow followed by arctic air. The entire precinct closely watched the weather report. A tradition in Iowa passed down from generations who spent their lives working the land, always eyeing the sky. But every cop knew how much the climate determined, the trouble it could cause.

First Watch had always been Heath's preference. They called it the Graveyard—a shift both deathly boring and one that brought out the dead. Except Heath liked the strangeness of the nighttime world, all those tweakers and drunks. They somehow seemed like the kind of people he could help most, even if it was by force. Sherry had warned him to take up another shift, a different sector, something closer to normal. That he was sheriff now and could spend his last years working daylight hours: safe and warm behind a desk. But this was his city, his beat. To give up that kind of territory felt like running away. And he'd had enough of that lately.

So tonight, sitting and waiting in his cruiser—feeling, once again, close to useless—Heath decided to call the Iowa City precinct, request Missing Persons, and ask for a little favor.

The rusted-out SUV with a broken taillight. A primer-coated Chevy weaving in his lane. The low-rider with booming bass. Always easier to profile the car than the driver. But each one checked out. No drunks. No arrests. Just a single ticket at midnight. A warning on expired tags at zero-one-hundred hours.

Heath filed each report, sent them on the MDT, and checked his phone.

No messages.

For years, he loved the idea of his family asleep while he kept the streets safe. But tonight he wondered if this was just some fantasy since Sherry was probably still awake, awaiting his return. Preparing to explain what happened this afternoon when he saw the bank statement and said there must've been a mistake. He was about to call the bank, cancel the tuition check he didn't write, when Sherry told him to hang up the phone. That she wrote it herself.

Three a.m. was the worst part of the night. Bar time come and gone, and nothing left but time on your hands. Heath didn't wish for bad things to happen, but slow shifts bred other problems. Put your guard down—that's exactly when the bad things happened. Except tonight, though Heath tried to keep the thoughts at bay, time just wouldn't leave him alone.

Like why Maria Diaz's mother took so long to report. Three hours made the difference between missing and lost. How many miles could be covered, how far could someone run, with a head start like that? And what kind of mom wouldn't say anything until it was possibly too late?

But maybe it wasn't for him to say. When his daughter was young, he'd get home just in time to see her make her way into the day. Then he'd wake for dinner, tuck her into bed, and walk out into the dark again. Even when Megan was in high school, he'd maybe take a morning run with her once a month. Catch a football game or two, watch her march in the band.

But doing the math, the minutes didn't add up to much.

Lately, even his shifts felt slippery, the seconds ticking so slow it seemed the sun would never rise, while other times the night snuck by him like a thief. The hours could mess with you if you let them. Instead it was best to keep on driving, knowing that, if nothing else, simply moving forward was sometimes the only way to fight the clock.

The gas station by the trailer court had been robbed twice in the last year, so Heath made it part of his rounds, even if it was all the way on the edge of town. But tonight the place was empty. He poured coffee and yelled a quick hello when he heard movement in back followed by a small whimper. Heath took a deep breath, ready to call for backup, when a girl appeared between the swinging doors, wiping her eyes. He'd seen her around town, but never working here before.

"What do you want?" she asked, her voice breaking on the last word.

Heath raised his coffee. Maybe it was the crying, but the girl looked exhausted. Her nametag read *Betsy*. She was little, almost a full foot shorter than him. "How's your night?"

"Two dollars." Brown hair bloomed from her ponytail. She couldn't have been much beyond high school, if that. "Hey, you guys arrest deadbeat dads, right?"

"Sometimes. If a judge tells us to."

"Do they ever let you arrest someone before they become a dad?"

Heath should've figured as much. Domestics were the worst. But he wasn't sure of the protocol here. It felt like he should stay; it felt like he should leave her alone.

Instead, he took a sip of coffee and wondered how far along she was.

"He's such an asshole," she said, like it was a simple fact.

"A little advice?" He was about to say *one parent to another* but caught himself.

Betsy put a tissue to her nose, attempted a small chuckle. "Is it that obvious?"

"Doing this job, I've learned not to judge people too fast. They may just surprise you."

"Seriously?" she said. "That's never been my experience."

Heath wasn't sure if she was referring to cops or fathers or something else entirely. But either way, he wasn't sure what it was about him that made every witness turn hostile tonight.

"Well, maybe it's *you* who needs to make a change. Like, say, your choice in men."

Her eyes, at first tired-looking, now quickened at the words. "Two dollars."

"I'm sorry. It's none of my—"

"Anything else I can help you with, sir?"

Forty-nine years old and almost half his life spent raising a daughter, Heath still had no idea how to talk to women, who always seemed to treat him like an enemy instead of a hero. Especially when all he wanted her to help him with was helping her—which was maybe why he reached across the counter, laid his hand on hers, and said, "You know, if you were my daughter—"

Betsy pulled her hand back as if burned. "I thought you were the good guys."

Heath's breath sharpened, out of anger or shame he wasn't sure. But as he held his wallet and pulled out two bills, his hands were shaking, something they never used to do on the job.

"Maybe you're right," he said, placing his money on the counter. "If a deadbeat isn't up for the job, you're probably better off without him."

Megan hadn't come home for Christmas. In fact, she rarely called at all her first semester, and if she did it was to talk to Sherry. It didn't seem strange, a girl needing her mom. But when break came and they didn't hear anything, Heath called her R.A. only to discover she'd moved out of the dorm.

So he put on a uniform and drove to Iowa City. After showing his badge around, he was led to a counselor who had seen his daughter around Halloween. Megan had been "struggling."

"With what?" he asked. "Why didn't she tell us?"

The counselor reassured him that was part of the problem. "Kids in crisis rarely reach out."

Crisis. Heath didn't know what to do with the word. But when he pressed the issue, the counselor claimed confidentiality. "But maybe you should talk to the roommate."

When he got to the dorm, a girl with pink hair opened the door.

He remembered moving Megan in, how happy she seemed

that day. But now the room was half-empty. A bed sat in the corner, stripped down to the mattress.

The roommate was named Evie. Her first words: "Too little, too late, don't you think?"

Heath felt like a criminal: an intruder in his own family. "Listen, do you know where—"

"What do you care?" she said.

"Excuse me?"

"Megan's starting a new life. With someone she loves."

"I see. So who is this guy?"

"See, that's the thing," Evie said with a grin. "There is no guy."

Heath waited for her to continue, the words not quite adding up, until she nodded at him, offering up a little wink.

"This isn't a joke, you know."

"Am I laughing?" she said, the smile still sitting on her face.

Heath wasn't sure what to believe anymore. But he did know he wasn't going to get a straight answer here. However, when the door started to shut, Heath couldn't help but stop it with his foot and say, "When you see my daughter, tell her I'm looking for her. Can you do that?"

"Aren't you listening, man?" They shared a long stare until finally the smile fell from her lips. The girl couldn't even look him in the eye when Heath took his foot away, allowing the door to quietly close.

That afternoon, with no other lead, Heath went to the Iowa City precinct. Except his daughter was of age. She wasn't technically "missing." Plus, it wasn't his jurisdiction, forcing him to drive back without any answers. Except when he got home and told his wife about their daughter living with a woman, something he still couldn't process, Sherry seemed relieved.

"She's okay then."

Heath expected shock, or at the very least some questions.

Some kind of concern they could share. "I don't know. The counselor said she was in crisis."

"Crisis?" Sherry glared from across the kitchen. "Why do you think she got a counselor?"

Heath shrugged. "She's confused."

"Who's confused, Heath?"

"Our daughter. I think she's a little lost."

"I don't know," Sherry said, slowly walking toward him. When he saw the tears puddling in her eyes, Heath held out his arms, eager to comfort someone. But Sherry stopped short of him, keeping her distance. "Maybe she's just scared."

"Scared? Scared of what?"

"How could you not know?"

"You tell me. You seem to have all the answers."

"No," she hissed, raising her hand so that Heath couldn't help but flinch. But instead his wife gently touched his face and whispered, "I mean, how could you not know?"

It was the only time they talked about it. And though Sherry never specifically used the word *blame*, Heath almost wished she had. At least then there'd be some kind of answer to agree upon: case closed. Instead, Sherry became another missing person in his life. She lay in bed for days. They didn't celebrate Christmas. Without Meg, it seemed strange to keep up appearances.

Then, a week later, on New Year's Eve, Heath woke to his wife singing, laughing to herself. He wondered if depression had turned to hysteria. If she was finally on the verge of a meltdown. But when she suggested a date night before his shift, he decided to take any kind of forgiveness granted him. Plus, the idea of putting the year behind them felt too good to pass up.

While waiting for a table and not talking—what could be said that they didn't already know about each other?—they ran into some old neighbors, which at first seemed fortunate. Like maybe a double date would help them see who they used to be. But five minutes into the conversation, their friends brought up kids, how they grew up so fast. Heath was about to change the subject when they asked about Megan. "Don't tell me she's already in college?"

It was hard to believe they didn't know. That there were actual parents in the world with kids who grew up like they were supposed to. Heath imagined their reactions when he broke the news. How he'd forever look different in the eyes of these people who'd only known him one way their entire lives. But before he could speak, Sherry smiled and took his hand.

"Sure is. Moved out and doing great. I think she's finally happy." Then Sherry gave another laugh, touched a tear in the corner of her eye. "I mean, you know, to be on her own."

The neighbor chuckled. "Who knew we'd miss them when they're gone? Am I right?"

"It's true." Heath nodded and squeezed his wife's hand. "Who knew?"

When the Camry was clocked going eighty, a blur of white flying across Highway 20, Heath flashed his cherries. When it didn't slow down, he was ready to run the plates—if the numbers hadn't been hidden behind snowpack. So Heath hit the siren, preparing for a high-speed pursuit, when the Camry simply pulled over. Almost always a sign of someone with nothing to hide.

Heath put his frustration aside, prepared to give the guy a ticket and get back to work. But when he knocked on the window, there was no response. The man just sat there, staring out the windshield. It took a second knock before the glass eventually rolled down.

"Do you know why I pulled you over?" But his question was met with silence.

Heath quickly swept the interior, asked for registration,

when his flashlight beam landed on the gun, its barrel sticking out beneath the driver's seat.

Heath rarely had to draw his firearm, but now he placed a hand on the holster, unclasped its leather latch. "Put your hands on the wheel."

The man had already complied but said nothing.

"Is the gun loaded, sir?"

He gripped his Glock, finger on the trigger, when he heard a Mexican accent say: "Bebé!"

"Who else is in the car with you, sir?"

"Bebé," the man repeated.

Heath told him to get out, place his hands on the hood.

But it only took a once-over to tell there was no little girl waiting to be saved. And when he reached under the seat, the gun was far lighter than it looked.

The car was registered to David Cruz, a man without even one outstanding ticket. Heath wrote up a warning and returned the BB gun. "Take this home. Comprende?"

The man shook his head and said, "Mi niño's."

"I don't care whose it is. You shouldn't have it in your car."

David Cruz pointed at the barrel. "És bebé."

"I know," Heath said. "But it doesn't look like...just give it back to your boy, okay?"

He walked away before having to explain himself again, feeling both disappointed and relieved. The man wasn't any abductor. Just a dad trying to get home to his kids. But David Cruz was also lucky. He'd never know how close he came to seeing a real gun tonight. Heath sat in the cruiser, hands still shaking, as he watched the man slip back behind the wheel of the Camry, but not before placing the BB gun right back beneath the driver's seat.

Maybe the crisis started last spring when he arrested the two boys. Heath didn't discuss work, but Megan's senior year was coming to an end. She was old enough now. Plus, he wanted her to hear it from him first. There'd be rumors and he wanted to get the facts straight for her. So as Meg ate cereal and his wife sipped coffee, Heath explained his call to the football field. Kids loitering and up to no good. "And wasn't that the truth," he said, trying to put a smile on the incident.

"What were they doing?" Sherry asked, carefully eyeing their daughter.

"What weren't they doing? I pull up to the field, figuring they'd run away. Probably not even worth the paperwork. But when I turn on my lights, there're two boys, tangled up and tripping over their pants." Heath shook his head, laughing to himself. "So I put them in back. Call parents. It was a mess. No charges. But those boys are going to have it rough today."

Heath sat back, hoping his daughter was smart enough to fill in the blanks.

And it turned out she did. Just the wrong ones.

Four in the morning: a lead. White Camry with matching plates. Last seen at a drive-thru in Des Moines. After the alert, the restaurant manager reviewed the security footage. No visual, except the driver ordered a kid's meal. It was hours ago—but also a chance Maria Diaz was still in the state.

The sun was on its way, first shift almost done with nothing to show for it. On busy nights, he'd be breaking up bar fights, dropping in on noise complaints, dealing with Domestics, so at times Heath felt more like a babysitter than a sheriff, giving time-outs to drunken children.

But tonight there'd be little paperwork, which was usually a blessing. Though now it also meant he'd have to go home that much sooner, listen to Sherry fill him in on the details. All the things she started to tell him yesterday. About the call she received two weeks ago, on New Year's Eve. Their daughter still in Iowa City and needing a tuition check because of the hold on her account. How she moved in with an older girl, some grad student named Lucìa Torres. They met at a rally and Megan couldn't help it. She was in love. His daughter was in love and didn't want him to know. In fact, begged Sherry to not say a word about it.

"Why not?" he asked. It felt like a prank—some trick on the old man. Except he saw from his wife's face that it was the whole truth and nothing but. "What kind of bullshit is she getting herself into?"

"Right there," Sherry had said, shaking her head. "That's why."

"C'mon, I didn't mean it that way." But there was no convincing anyone. Not anymore. So when he left to get some air, Heath decided to grab his gun belt and get to work instead.

Except now Heath wondered how he did mean it. At first, it was just the bullshit of college filling Megan's head with ridiculous ideas. Or the bullshit of this new girl poisoning the well: someone who probably protested everything, including cops.

Heath couldn't stop thinking about that word—crisis—and how earlier tonight Sherry tried to tell him about the point of college, about finding yourself. *Identity crisis*. A bullshit excuse. Heath found out who he was at eighteen, first by signing up for the Army followed by the police academy—always striving to protect and serve, one way or another.

So, perhaps, people just bullshit themselves into thinking they know somebody, only to find out they're someone else. Maybe always have been. Still, it doesn't stop you from wanting that first person back.

He blinked away the idea and added up the time. Three more hours before calling it quits. And though it wasn't his jurisdiction—but needing to be needed tonight—Heath took an hour-long detour to Des Moines. The cold had driven everyone indoors. So the only people left on the road were cops like him, each searching for one white car: a solitary flake buried in a snowbank.

***

Though no charges were filed, the football field soon became part of his rounds. And even if no kids had returned since, Heath had been right about one thing: the boys did have a tough time.

Megan told him about graffiti on lockers and punches in the showers.

"Can't you do something?" she asked one afternoon.

He'd just woken up and was eating breakfast while she made lunch. "Anyone report it?"

Meg shook her head. "They can't."

"Why can't they?" But Heath had seen enough to know that reporting in a small town only made things worse. "If they don't ask for help, it's out of my hands."

She took a bite out of her sandwich, carefully chewed it. "But you're responsible."

Heath pounded the table hard enough to make Megan's plate topple to the floor. The sound of it shattering filled the room. "Did I tell those kids to trespass? Act indecent in public?"

"Indecent?" Megan hadn't stopped chewing, unfazed by the shards on the floor.

"That was the charge."

Megan crossed her arms and turned her attention to the kitchen window, as if studying her own reflection.

"And it was dropped," he said. "So they were lucky."

Megan smiled into the glass and quietly whispered, "Lucky."

They sat in silence until she finally bent down to clean up the mess from the floor.

"Listen," Heath said, watching her walk across the kitchen and place the cracked plate in the garbage. "I was just doing my job."

"That's strange," she said, picking up two fragments and gently fitting them together.

"What's strange?"

"I thought your job was to protect people," she said before throwing the broken pieces back into the trash.

Des Moines was a dead end. The sun came up, the shift officially coming to an end, and Heath was ready to head back to Dexton when his cell phone rang.

"Sheriff Sawyer? Missing Persons in Iowa City returning your call."

"Did you find the place?" Heath asked.

"We stopped by the residence of Lucìa Torres. As you requested."

"And was my daughter there?"

"So this was a favor. Nothing official. We had no real authority to be there."

"Did you find her or not?"

"She wasn't missing. Okay? You need to understand that."

"So you talked to her. Is she okay?"

"Sheriff Sawyer, she made it pretty clear that..."

"What? What did she say?"

"Listen, it's not really our place to get involved in Domestics."

Heath wanted to hang up, wished he'd never made the call. So this is what people meant when they said no news is good news, the comfort that comes from not knowing.

"Did you tell her it was me? Who sent you to find her?"

"Sir, sometimes people just don't want to be found."

The phone shook in his hand, and Heath felt the unmistakable wobble in his voice when he said, "But that's my job."

He only half-heard the rest. Something about harassment charges, threat of a restraining order. None of it serious—all emotion. To just give it time. That some space may help. But before he could take any more advice, Heath hung up on him, mid-sentence.

He watched the sun rise over the city, and like most mornings, thought about that last run.

Megan had always been a good girl. Okay grades. Reliable friends. Went to bed early so she could wake before dawn to exercise. She ran track but never first heat. Still, he'd sometimes join her after his shift. They'd jog slow enough to talk. A book she'd read, a band she liked. But the day before she moved out, they went an extra mile, then two.

"Excited about college?" he asked, hoping the workout would last forever.

Megan shrugged. And neither said another word until they ran past the high school. Then Megan abruptly stopped, perhaps waiting for him to catch up. The sun had just crested the horizon, washing the sky with light. But when Heath finally drew near, panting with his hands on his hips, he could no longer see his daughter. It was as if someone new had taken her place, a stranger staring out at the fifty-yard line and barely breaking a sweat.

In the deep glow of daybreak, Heath felt invisible next to her, making him wonder if this was the version of his daughter that others saw. And if they knew that what they saw was beautiful.

"Dad?"

Heath startled at the word. Even her voice felt unfamiliar. "Yeah, honey?"

Megan studied the football field, as if talking to herself. "Never mind."

He was always curious what she'd wanted to tell him, figuring it was just nerves about leaving home. Leaving him. But of course now he knew it had nothing to do with him. And everything to do with him. His little girl was scared. And now, this morning, looking at the city skyline, he wondered if she had the right to be. He wasn't sure if he was more upset at her betrayal—keeping secrets from him when he'd done so much for her, loved her beyond love—or if maybe it was the entire idea of love that bothered him. How it never worked the way it was supposed to. As if desertion was always a natural part of it, no matter what you did or didn't do.

Either case, right now, going home only meant things getting worse before getting better.

And he wasn't ready for worse yet. He needed some better. So when the report came in about a white Camry on the south side of the city, Heath hit his sirens and ran the reds, hoping the streets were empty enough that they could lead him to a little lost girl, unharmed.

The zoo was still open, despite the cold. They had indoor exhibits all winter: insects, plants, birds in the aviary. Today, when Heath arrived, the lot was almost empty: two school buses idling near the entrance—and a little white car parked like an island surrounded by a sea of asphalt.

Backup hadn't arrived and, though it broke procedure, Heath refused to wait around for help; couldn't stand the thought of another child giving him the slip.

At the entrance, two women dressed in khaki from head to toe told him they were last seen walking through the aquarium, heading outside. But there was a special penguin program today. Students from around the district had been invited.

"How many?" Heath asked.

One of the zookeepers shrugged. "Two schools came. Maybe fifty kids. They're on the terrarium tour."

"Good. Keep them inside."

They nodded and pointed him to the penguins.

Outside, the air was warmer. The cold front had come to an end, leaving a tolerable chill, though Heath could still see his breath as he wandered the paths. He wasn't sure what to expect at the end of the trail, but abductions reeked of desperation. And desperate meant unpredictable. As he ran under the arch plastered with cartoon fish, Heath rested a hand on his sidearm. He scaled his way around the circular enclosure, penguins swirling through its waters, until two murky shadows appeared on the other side of the glass. Heath unclipped the leather clasp again, clicked off the safety, and turned the corner, expecting to see some kind of monster.

Instead, it was simply a man holding a little girl's hand.

For a moment, Heath hesitated—something he'd been trained to never do—as he watched the father point into the tank. The girl squinted and then squealed at the sight of two penguins swimming in tandem.

"Sir." Heath heard reluctance in the word. "Sir! Back away from the child."

The dad jumped at Heath's voice as it echoed around the empty space.

The girl's smile disappeared. She sounded close to tears when she whispered, "Papá?"

The father didn't let go of her hand.

"I need you to put your hands where I can see them, sir. And back up from the child."

"Are we in trouble?" the girl asked.

The man crouched down to look her in the eye. "No, m'ija. We're just fine."

"Are you going to jail?"

"Sir, I'm going to need you to—"

The man held up his hand, as if Heath were interrupting.

"I told you I can't skip school," she said. "It's my fault."

"No, cariño, it's mine. And no one's going to jail." The father brushed the girl's hair from her face, offered a weak smile. "I'm right here. Papá's not going anywhere. Ever. Okay?"

"Okay." She took a deep breath, the color returning to her face.

Heath wondered if the man actually believed his own lie when he gave his daughter a quick wink and stood back up. "Listen," he said. "I don't know what's—"

"There's a warrant, sir. You're going to have to come with me."

"Okay, okay. No problem. Can't we just—"

"Now, sir."

"Hey, just let me..." the man said, taking several steps toward Heath. It wasn't really a threat. More an attempt to strike a deal, negotiate. But Heath had had about enough compromising. At least enough to unholster his gun for the second time in a single shift.

"Don't move," Heath said, pointing the gun to the floor. "Stay right there."

The father halted, held up his hands.

All Heath had to do was put on the cuffs. Arrest the man, save the girl. But then there were those eyes: wide and wet and staring at her dad as if for the last time. She was terrified, and Heath was the reason why. He was her worst nightmare.

The man's hands still hung in the air, unsure of what to do. "Can't I just drive her home?"

"I can't let you do that," Heath said, the gun shaking in his hands. "You shouldn't have taken her in the first place."

"I just wanted some time." He shrugged like a scolded boy. "And she loves penguins."

Heath stared into the glass partition. The water looked cold and empty until a penguin raced by, coming into focus and then diminishing into the distance. The enclosure seemed smaller than it should be, claustrophobic for animals that were so obviously bred for open waters. But maybe they were happier caged up. At least they were protected. Locked up tight for their own good. Except as he watched the black-and-white blurs swim back and forth behind the glass, Heath couldn't help but wonder, if this was love, why it looked so much like punishment.

Heath took a deep breath, relaxed his shoulders. Part of him wanted to apologize. But a requirement of the job was to never say sorry. To admit wrongdoing put everything at risk.

"Listen, I'll tell you what I'll do." The suspect's eyes widened with hope until Heath quickly added, "But first, I need you to put your hands behind your back."

The man looked at his daughter and said, "C'mon. Is that really—"

"That's the deal," Heath said, holstering his firearm and taking out the cuffs.

The man looked down at his feet. "Fine."

"Listen up," Heath said, clicking the metal strands tight around his wrists. "You have about two minutes before this place is swarming with people like me. And they won't be doing you any favors. So my advice is to take this time and tell her what she needs to hear."

But when the man bent back down, unable to offer any hugs this time, the girl at last saw through the lies. She didn't even try to fight the tears anymore, and Heath couldn't stand the sight of it. Instead, he slowly backed up around the bend of the aquarium, never letting his eyes off them. And through the thick curve of glass, he caught a glimpse of a daughter putting her arms around a father's neck, telling him it was okay, Daddy. That we all make mistakes sometimes. Or at least that's what he hoped. Except Heath would never know for sure because by the time he'd turned the corner she was already too far away for him to hear her.

REPLACEMENT PARTS

Madeline Davis-Dempsey entered our second-grade class with magic hair. Her first day at Bridger Elementary, she appeared to be another quiet kid, shiny black curls hanging to her waist. However, the next day it was cropped like a boy's and almost white under the bright fluorescents. By the end of the week, she had a bright blue ponytail that swung back and forth like bait to a little boy's grasp, just begging to be pulled. Except nobody dared touch it, that thick braid too strange for our hands to hold. And though Madeline could change her hair overnight like a tooth fairy's visit, no one really thought about the reason, and she never gave any explanation—until, of course, she didn't come to school for weeks at a time.

Then I'd look from next door, through my bedroom window into hers, our houses so alike yet not. When she wasn't in Mrs. Hoover's class, Madeline lay in bed all day. Her head—bare and bald and full of sleep—sank into the pillow as I memorized each detail. Her walls were painted pink while mine stayed as boring as the day I was born. Her scalp, white and smooth like a newly-stitched softball. And then that row of colorful hair sitting atop fake heads, lining her room in a way that reminded me of the rainbows that came when looking at light through glass.

***

Last summer, when the Davis-Dempseys moved in with our elderly neighbor, my folks wouldn't let me go visit. "Her daughter isn't well," my mom said. "You don't need to be around that, okay?"

I said okay but still wondered if Madeline was so sick then why, out of all the places on Earth, had her mom brought her to Bridger? "Where did they come from, anyway?"

"Back East," my dad said. "Wouldn't surprise me if she has some stuck-up accent now."

Back East—the words felt life-size in my mouth.

"I think she became a professor too," Mom said. "Just like her father."

"What's that mean?" I asked.

"It's just a fancy word for teacher," Dad said.

I couldn't imagine any of the teachers at Bridger Elementary living "Back East." I thought about Mrs. Hoover having an accent and almost laughed out loud.

Except when I first saw Madeline reading on her patio and catching the last of the summer sun, she didn't look ill. Skinny and pale maybe, but still strong for the most part. In fact, she looked like a character out of a comic book, one of those girl-villains from exotic countries who had razor-blade noses and long legs. And though Madeline was scrawny and a bit tired-looking, she was still lovely in a way that felt so far away, even if she did live next door.

And I knew right then she wasn't dangerous or diseased but something else entirely.

It was an unspoken promise, a show of loyalty between us, that when new kids arrived we didn't invite them to birthdays, never shared seats on the bus, refused to even learn their names. But when it came to Madeline Davis-Dempsey, there was how she already knew what notes were called in music class. How she played piano while we were just beginning to puff on recorders. In gym, while jumping rope, Madeline taught us double-dutch, the hypnotic chants stuck in our heads all afternoon. The day we learned to count in Spanish, Madeline whispered something under her breath, and Mrs. Hoover made her repeat it, like maybe it was a dirty word. But when Madeline spoke again, using sounds that weren't really words except to Mrs. Hoover, we all sat slack-jawed—as if the girl's voice had suddenly become possessed by some invisible spirit.

So though we tried, nobody could forget her name. She was impossible to ignore. Until one afternoon at recess when she told us about being homeschooled. None of us believed her.

"Before we moved here, my mom quit teaching college kids and taught me instead." She sat high up on the monkey bars, her orange hair twisting down like it was on fire. "Only me."

"You're making it up," Tim Richards said, squinting at her like she was the sun.

"It's true, Tim. We even went on field trips. Every week."

"You can't even do that. It's against the law."

Everyone nodded. But Madeline just smiled, flipped down between the bars and hung from bent legs. And those orange curls—that long chameleon hair we never questioned though it was always on the back of our minds—spilled below her head, swayed in the air, and dropped to the ground like little flames falling. I wanted to turn away and go on imagining about it, but instead we all just stared as if discovering for the first time she wasn't like us.

Madeline swung down and picked up the small puddle of orange fuzz. Then she carefully placed it back on her head and looked at everyone, her eyes full of water.

"What are you looking at?" she cried.

But none of us knew what to say about that.

***

Every Christmas, during Sunday school, the pastor's wife took out a giant strand of yarn and told us we were going to learn about God's love. She tied a key to the string as the entire class linked elbows. We were supposed to work together to weave the key through our arms without breaking the chain. There were some nervous laughs when the boys had to touch the girls, but despite our efforts, we could never do it before the hour was up. The pastor's wife said that was okay, trying was the important part, which led to her last-minute talk about our fellow man. How we were all connected, equally beautiful in God's eyes. Bound in brotherhood, woven together so that each tug of the strand, for good or bad, affects the way the world works. But when she asked if we had any questions, we were always too busy untangling ourselves from each other to ask.

It was spirit week, so we had to dress up as our future. Most boys wore hand-me-down uniforms from the factory, our dads' names stitched to the front, each of us swallowed by their size, while most girls carried dolls and called themselves Mom. All except Madeline, who entered class wearing nothing but scarves. We could barely even see her eyes peeking out beneath a shawl.

"A gypsy isn't really a career, Maddy," Mrs. Hoover said.

"My mom said I can be anything I want."

"Of course, dear." The teacher frowned. "I'm sure you'll make a great one someday."

But during recess, Tim started in on her again. "My mom said gypsies don't believe in Jesus. That it's just another word for a crook. People who hide behind rags on their heads."

The whole class grinned. For weeks, ever since her hair fell to the ground, we'd given Madeline the silent treatment.

But today she couldn't be unseen anymore, which was a clear challenge to the rules. A threat to the laws of our land. So, now, a lesson had to be taught.

Everyone nervously waited to see what Madeline would do next, secretly hoping she'd just agree and walk away. Instead, she had more questions. "Tim, did you know that gypsies can see the future just by looking at people?"

"So?" he said, tugging the dirty ball cap over his eyes.

"Well," Madeline said, staring him right in the face. "Your future is looking real ugly."

Tim's cheeks became splotchy, as if a sudden rash had been inflamed. And when his fist tightened, the entire class was curious if he'd actually hit a girl, though we'd been told from the time we could walk that it was a cowardly thing to do. But Tim didn't seem to care. Beating his knuckles into an open palm like a catcher's mitt, it was as if the rules had changed so that maybe wrong sometimes meant right. Madeline hadn't moved except to cross her arms, the faintest trace of a smile visible beneath her veil. She was so calm, I had to wonder: if we were all supposed to be connected together, where did Madeline stand in the web of the world? And how would it impact all of us if nobody did anything? Which was maybe why I moved out of the crowd, forced my body between the two of them, and held up my hand like a crossing guard.

"You don't know what you're doing," I said, since it sounded like words our pastor shouted on Sundays.

"No, Geoff. *You* don't know what *you're* doing." Tim poked a finger at my chest. "She your girlfriend or something?"

Everyone *oohed* and *ahhed*. But when I turned around, Madeline was gone, vanished as if she'd been a ghost all along.

And though I didn't throw the initial punch, both of us were suspended for two days since in our school defending yourself got you in just as much trouble as taking that first swing.

***

Despite the suspension and black eye, my folks said they couldn't afford to take a day off. So that morning, after Dad left for the factory, Mom *kissed my ouchie better* before heading to the diner. Then, just a few moments later, Madeline arrived at my front door with a cardboard box. "I have something for you."

"Why aren't you at school?"

"My mom wanted me to go. She says school is the place I need to be right now. But my grandfather said it was best to stay home. Until things quieted down."

"My parents aren't here."

"Perfect," she said, walking past me. "Mom said it was okay to come over."

I figured one parent saying yes was as good as the next. So I followed her into the family room where she took a seat on the floor, her black bangs almost shrouding her eyes.

"Actually, my mom thought coming here was a great idea. She really approves of you."

I'd only seen Mrs. Davis-Dempsey from a distance through my window. Her hair was so short that each time she came into her daughter's room it was hard to tell the two of them apart.

"There's something important we need to talk about." Madeline placed the cardboard box between us. "And the fact is I think you're more of a spring than an autumn."

"A what?"

Madeline reached toward my face, but I pulled away before she could touch it.

"Your complexion doesn't fit." She shook her head as if disappointed in whoever messed up making me. "This seems more your style."

She pulled a pink wig out of the box.

"Maddy, I don't think my parents would like me wearing that."

"Call me Madeline," she said, combing through the wig. "Mom says to always keep true to my real name. Even if most people want the other version."

"Is that why you have two last names? One for each version?"

"Exactly, Geoffrey." Madeline smiled. "I think we should use your full name too, just between us. It's more gallant, don't you think? Noble."

I'd read books about bravery and virtue, but nobody had ever used words like that to describe me. I pointed at my eye and said, "Does pink go with black?"

"They're a perfect complement." Madeline lifted the wig. "May I?"

I lowered my head as she gently placed the wig over my hair.

"I hereby christen you Sir Geoffrey."

But I didn't really feel any different. In fact, it wasn't until Madeline leaned forward and placed her lips on my bruise that I felt, at last, fully reborn.

That winter Madeline snuck over to my house for a few minutes every day after school, bearing gifts. Sometimes she brought more wigs, each with a different job. Blonde wigs meant we were surfers living in a place with beaches and sun and no such thing as snow. Red hair and we'd be spies on a mission. When I asked her who we were fighting, she'd say Bridger was full of secret terrorists. But sometimes she brought other things—games, tarot cards, books. She read giant volumes of fairy tales. Girls losing their way in the woods, eating poisoned apples right and left. Always getting locked up in towers, waiting for that one guy who'd finally climb their walls.

One day, I simply had to interrupt. "Why is everyone in these stories so horrible?"

"What are you talking about?" she asked. "I wish all bullies got their eyes plucked out."

"I guess." At school, everyone had stopped talking to me now that I sat with Madeline for lunch, played with her at recess. It was the only time we could be together in public and not worry about the eyes of parents. "I just don't know why they're so mean in the first place?"

"Because they're weak."

"The mean people? Or the ones they're mean to?"

"Exactly, Geoffrey."

I wasn't sure which she agreed with, so I just nodded as if I understood. Like maybe it meant I was the strong one. And it felt nice to be on that side of things for once.

I tapped the edge of her book. "It must be scary being a kid in that world."

"It is." Madeline flipped the page. "They always seem to be a problem, don't they?"

"But I don't know why. They never do anything wrong."

"Yes, they do. They ruin everyone's plans. They're constantly in the way." Madeline softly closed the book. "But in the end, everyone gets what they deserve."

"And they all live happily ever after."

"No. It never says that," Madeline said, pulling off the purple wig to expose her bald head. "When each story's over, it just says 'The End.'"

I took the wig from her hands and put it on my head, trying to make her laugh. To show that she didn't need a disguise around me. But when she didn't even crack a smile, I decided it was time to show her there was nothing to fear. I cradled the warm skin of her scalp, perfectly round like a crystal ball, pulling me into its trance. And though at first she flinched, it wasn't long before her eyes closed, as if a kiss from a prince was the only thing she needed to break the curse. It was the first time I'd taken a girl in my hands and touched her lips to mine, so I was hoping she'd know what to do next. But Madeline simply sat there, still as a photograph, and I knew this had never happened to her either, making me feel like I was the one with the magic. The power to heal. But before I could pull back to see if I'd fixed anything at all, the front door swung open, letting in the sunlight and the cold air and the shadow of my father who made a small noise as he ran across the room and tore the wig from my head. Then he carried me off like an ogre does a damsel in distress. But over his shoulder I could still see Madeline on the floor, silent and hairless, her head bowed as if patiently awaiting the swift fall of the sword.

On Valentine's Day, we had to dance with a girl so our parents could watch. For the recital, Tim and I were paired with Alice Sorenson, since there weren't enough girls to go around anymore. Madeline hadn't been in school lately, and I'd been grounded, so we hadn't seen each other for weeks. Until one day at rehearsals she showed up as if out of nowhere. Mrs. Hoover suggested it best for her to sit and watch. When asked why, the teacher said there wasn't enough time to teach her the steps. So Madeline started to walk offstage, tucking herself away in the wings of the auditorium, until I raised my hand and said, "I could be her coach."

And suddenly I was leading Madeline Davis-Dempsey in circles. Her bird-bone hand clasped in mine, her feet almost floating above the floor. She asked me to twirl her faster, spinning like a glass girl on top of a music box, but it wasn't long before she began to wobble. Her head flopped about as if detached from her neck. The green wig flew through the air. And though her voice kept saying to *speed up*, eventually she let go, her body collapsing to the floor. I tried to hold on, tried to catch her before she fell. But in the end, I just wasn't fast enough.

Mrs. Hoover told someone to get the nurse, to get the principal, to call 911.

However, it wasn't long before Madeline's eyes seemed to

be opening, blinking fast, as if she was about to stand up at any second to tell us it was simply too much fun for her to take.

"Mrs. Hoover," I said. "She just lost her footing. It's my fault."

"Okay, kids," the teacher said, clapping her hands. "Line up and head back to the room."

"Just let her rest a second," I said. "She's fine."

"I knew this was a bad idea." Mrs. Hoover frantically fanned Madeline's face. "Geoff. Please, go back with the class. You don't need to see her like this."

"I'm the *only* one who sees her," I yelled, stomping my foot on the ground.

"You're out of line, young man," she said, giving me a no-nonsense glare. "Now, go with the class or go to detention."

"No!" It was the first time I ever talked back to an adult. So my face felt like a furnace as I pointed a finger at her and said, "Nobody's leaving. Turn on the music. And let's try it again."

When our teacher's eyes softened, it almost seemed like she would do as told, as if truly under my spell, until Mrs. Hoover whispered something about Jesus Christ, laid Madeline's head back against the floor, and breathed deeply into the sleeping girl's mouth.

I spent the afternoon staring through my window at an empty room. The outlines of her wigs sat alone in the dark. Her bed was still made. Nothing moved in the house for hours, until the sun completely sank, and I gave up to go help Mom bake cookies for our classroom party tomorrow.

Dad sat looking through the Want Ads while my mom rolled dough for another batch. Dad said the factory was lay-ing off people, which at first sounded like a good thing. Like free vacations for a job well done. But he'd been in a bad mood the last week, so today I took a bite out of one of the baked hearts and wondered if I was still in trouble. Especially since there hadn't been any mention of detention after Madeline was rushed out of the auditorium on a stretcher.

Mom said *Don't spoil your dinner*, and I asked when we'd visit Madeline. "She likes cookies."

"Honey, I know you mean well, but I don't think it's a good idea."

"But in church, we always talk about doing unto others. Why don't we ever do that?"

She sprinkled flour on the rolling pin and eyed my dad, who simply ruffled his pages.

"Son," he said. "Sometimes no matter how much you do for others, it doesn't do any damn good."

"So helping people doesn't always help people."

"Sometimes," my mom interrupted, placing a cookie sheet in the oven.

"Well, then why doesn't the Bible say that?"

"Don't talk back to your mother," my dad said, his face still buried in the folds of the paper. "Someday, when you're older, this will all make more sense."

"How does it make sense to *not* visit someone in the hospital?" I asked.

Mom handed me the timer and told me to set it for fifteen minutes. Then she poured me a glass of milk and said, "Maddy just needs to be with her family right now."

"But aren't they our neighbors? Doesn't that make them our family?"

"No." Dad dropped his paper, casting a look at my mom. "It makes them our neighbors."

"Stop it, Carl. Don't listen to him, honey. Maddy just needs some time alone, okay?"

"Fine." Except Mom must've heard something else in my voice because she quickly wrapped her arms around me and said I had the biggest heart. That I was the best kind of boy.

***

The next day, when Madeline wasn't in school, Mrs. Hoover made us write special Valentines for her to get well soon. When I put mine in her paper mailbox, Mrs. Hoover said, "Don't you live next door?" Before I could answer, she put a hand on my shoulder like I was going on a secret mission. "Will you deliver Maddy's cards? I'd hate to have them sitting here forever."

The idea of forever felt scary. But I also knew that was part of being one of the good guys. Courage came with the territory—even if it meant being grounded over and over.

So after school, I went straight from the bus to Madeline's front door. I hadn't been near the house since they'd moved in, and it felt like I'd somehow entered a foreign country without permission. Figuring nobody was home, I tried to stuff the entire box through the door's mail slot. When it wouldn't fit, I started to slip each card through, one at a time, until the door pulled away and there stood Madeline's mother. We stared at each other, confused by the moment. Her eyes looked puffy, as if she'd just woken up—or hadn't slept yet. But after seeing the Valentine in my hand, she swung open the door and said, "Please. Come in."

I followed her to the kitchen table where she took my coat and served me heart-shaped cookies. "Your mother dropped these by earlier. Such a nice woman. Always offering food."

I wasn't sure if she was talking about the right person until I tasted a cookie and knew it could only be my mom's.

"I forgot that part about Iowa. Casseroles cure anything." She laughed to herself. "Cookies and prayer. That's all it takes."

"Did you used to live here, Mrs. Davis-Dempsey?"

"It's just Dempsey now," she corrected, shaking her head. "My daughter refuses to give up her dad's name. Even after he gave up on us."

"Did he die?"

"Not yet," she said with a smile. "Ben and I are just separated. But he still lives in Iowa City, with his new tenure-track job, while I came back here. Grew up in this house, actually."

"What was that like?" I asked, curious if the town I knew was the same one as hers.

"Place felt smaller then. Once upon a time. Then one day I just left it all behind." She slid a napkin across the table. "Went halfway around the world. On a mission trip to help sick kids."

"Like a doctor."

"Not really. And it didn't do much good. Just made me relieved that I didn't have a child." She picked up a cookie and stared at it before putting it back down. "So I went back to school for a long time to become a different kind of doctor—until I got pregnant again. Twenty years later, and here came Madeline, unexpected as a miracle."

"What kind of doctor's not a doctor?"

"I teach World Theology."

"What's that?"

"It's looking at different myths and religions."

"You mean church stories?"

"Exactly," she said. "Tales we tell, trying to make sense of things that don't make sense."

"Your daughter has lots of tales to tell. They don't always make sense, though."

"They never really do the trick, do they?" She glanced at her watch, twisting it on her wrist. "But for now I teach part-time at NCC. Which is also right back where I began."

"Sort of like a do-over."

Ms. Dempsey half-smiled, her eyes crinkling at the corners. "The more things change, the more they stay the same. Have you ever heard that?"

I shook my head. "That doesn't make sense either."

"No, it doesn't." She was speaking so softly it was hard to hear her. But it didn't seem like she was talking to me anyway. "It just means there's no escape."

"Well, I hope you guys never leave again. I like having neighbors."

"Me too," she said, staring into space. "But it's colder here than I remember. Quieter."

Then we both listened to the quiet for a while. I took another bite, my mouth dry without milk to wash it down. Finally, I said, "I just came to drop off cards for Madeline."

"Madeline." A full grin formed on her lips. "Hardly anyone calls her that."

"My mom is probably worried by now. So I should get back."

"No!" She sighed and said, "Sorry. It's been a long night. She's coming from Iowa City. I just came early to get the room ready. But I think she'd rather see you right now."

"She's getting out of the hospital?"

"We want her home." She brought a hand to her mouth, muffling her voice when she said, "But don't worry if she looks different. She's the same Madeline, right?"

"It's okay. I know all about it. Actually, I think she looks better without hair."

Without warning, Ms. Dempsey stood and pulled me from my seat, holding me close like we were about to dance. My arms hung to the side as she rocked back and forth. It felt strange but good, like letting a mosquito suck at your skin a little. As if it was the least I could do.

"I think so too," she said. "But she still insists on wearing those wigs."

"I like them. They let you pretend to be someone else."

"That's the problem." When I tried to pull away, she held me tighter, my face pressed flat to her belly. "It's like trying to replace a part of yourself that you lost—but won't ever return."

"It'll grow back, right?"

"I shaved my head too," she said. "In some religions it's a sign of devotion. But Madeline insisted I grow it back. Told me it's why people always get cursed at the end of the story."

"Because everyone always gets what they deserve?"

"No. She said because it's an act of selfishness. To give up on the gifts you've been given. But maybe you're right," she said, tears cracking her voice. "In other religions, it's just another way to punish. Or repent."

The shuddering waves of her breath almost put me to sleep, until she sucked in a quick lungful of air and held it. Her whole body went tense when she whispered, "They're here."

The garage door hummed against the house as she told me again not to be nervous.

Then the kitchen door opened, and two men walked in backwards, lifting a wheelchair.

When they turned, I barely recognized Madeline behind the plastic mask.

"Look, Madeline. Geoff brought cards from the whole class."

But her eyes didn't light up to see me. Instead, they reeled around as if loose in her head.

Ms. Dempsey laid a hand on my shoulder. "Why don't you help Ben put her to bed?"

"Gloria," said our elderly neighbor, who today looked so much older than before. "You sure that's necessary?"

"Dad, don't." She gripped my arm. "I want her to have a friend there when she wakes."

He nodded like on second thought it was a good idea as he pushed Madeline to the stairs.

When I mentioned going home again, Ms. Dempsey gave me a small shove. Her ex-husband said to follow him with the oxygen tank as he picked up his daughter, which made me wonder if this was the way she always got upstairs. Though I spied on her sleeping in bed, I never thought about how she actually got there, never realized she floated like a cloud in someone else's arms.

But when we entered her room, it was completely empty. Except for the bed, everything had been removed, as if I'd been observing an optical illusion the entire time.

Once Madeline was wrapped in crisp-clean sheets, her dad pulled up a chair. "You can wait here until she wakes up. Do you understand?"

I wanted to ask him where the wigs were, but was afraid of his answer.

After he left, I stared at Madeline. She looked like a statue—her skin pale and polished. Her breath was mushy. And she couldn't keep still, as if uncomfortable, possibly in pain. She kept clawing at her mask, like she had something to say. So I stood and slid the plastic from her mouth, craving that voice, longing to hear the words she wanted to share—even if it was a simple *thank you*. Or the sound of my name on her lips, telling me, *Exactly, Geoffrey*.

But she didn't say anything. Instead, she began to wheeze, her lids at last snapping open.

"Madeline," I said, looking into her eyes, those pupils like flat black discs. "It's me."

And though I figured it'd make her feel right at home, Madeline simply blinked like I was some stranger in a strange room.

"What do you need?" I asked.

Her chest heaved—those eyes stricken and searching for help.

"I'm right here. Tell me what to do."

Madeline clutched at her nightgown, then at the sheets, until at last grabbing my shirt. She almost pulled me into bed with her, and when she opened her mouth, all that came out was a low moan. There was no actual language behind her sounds, but I knew she was asking for something, even if it was hard to hear over the pulse in my ears, my heart flapping like a broken wing in my chest. So maybe it was her making those sad noises I never knew existed, or that hand trying to drag me down with her, or possibly it was just seeing everything hollow in a room that was once so full. But at that moment, the blood pumping through my head told me to get out of there, to run away as fast as I could. And, like any good boy, I did as I was told.

That night at the Valentine's program, I had to share Alice Sorenson with Tim, trading her off between dances. The gym was dark, but the stage was lit. In the front row, my folks gave me a thumbs-up like this was the proudest moment of my life. Mrs. Hoover shouted orders from the wings about staying in time and to keep smiling. "Remember, you're supposed to be having fun!" Then she'd appear after each dance and bow for the claps as if they were hers to take. But despite the crowd, there was a lack of bodies in the room—a space no amount of applause could fill.

Tim was about to finish his last routine with Alice, their feet falling in unison.

Except the more they turned in circles—both faces blurring into a single flash of teeth and shiny hair—the more I felt seasick. My head still throbbed from this afternoon.

Earlier today, when I sprinted through the front door and into my mom's arms, I couldn't catch my breath to speak. She asked what was wrong, but I could only shake my head, panting Madeline's name over and again like an incantation. Or a confession. Anything to help cast her out of my mind. My mom hugged me tight, but I could hear the tears in her voice when she said it wasn't anyone's fault. That it wasn't fair to ever have to feel this way.

But tonight, while still offstage, I wasn't sure what to feel. I didn't touch dinner and could still taste my mother's cookies on my tongue; the sweetness making my stomach turn. Sweat coated my skin like an unexpected fever. I'd never felt so tired in my life. So to stop the room from spinning, to find some kind of focus, I looked at my parents in the crowd.

Except instead of encouragement, their faces were filled with fright.

The music had come to an end. Everybody leaned forward in their chairs.

From the wings of the stage, I saw the class in their next position: exact rows of boy-girl, boy-girl, hands clasped and ready to line-dance. Tim was there as well, standing with Alice, waiting for me to take my place next to them.

The entire audience stared at me, wondering what I'd do next. *Was I going to be the one who messed it up? That kid who ruined the show for everyone?* But when Mrs. Hoover caught me in her sights, throwing me that don't-you-dare stare, my body started to relax, as if given a sudden permission. And when she mouthed the words *Follow directions*, I began to breathe easy again. Because though for a moment I was the odd man out, it didn't take long before I lowered my head and walked across the stage, everybody smiling as I finally got back in line.

ANYWHERE BUT IOWA

It was hard to sell my guns, handing them over to a pawnshop like second-rate scrap metal. A giant .357 as well as my father's Desert Eagle, a real collector's item he bought during his tour in Afghanistan. But with the charges pending and Christmas on the way, it seemed like the only thing to do. When I walked into Dexton Gun & Pawn on my lunch break, I figured the guy would hand over a wad of cash. Instead, he stared at the firearms as if they were nothing special.

A thick pane of scratched plastic stood between us. His face was slick with grease and the place smelled like dirty laundry. He didn't even bother to look up when he said, "Five hundred."

"Look at the serial number. Limited edition."

"Uh-huh." He took off his fat, black glasses. "Five hundred."

I told him they were easily worth double. Some people would probably pay even more.

"What are the chances I'm gonna sell a Limited Edition? Take a look around."

Broken appliances filled the shelves. Metal bars barricaded the windows like a jail cell.

In other words, the store was a real heap where you'd be

144

lucky if a customer had a mouthful of teeth, much less a dollar to spend. Dexton used to be a clean town until everything got siphoned off by the highway toward Bridger. Then the factory shut down, so now the only things left behind were a fully-stocked pawnshop and a bail bondsman who kept plenty busy. Last night the news reported more meth coming into the state. Even today, on the way to work, I saw a boarded-up building with *No Copper* painted across the door. It felt like I was driving through a different country, something third-world—anywhere but Iowa.

"I'm coming back for the Eagle," I told the clerk, who was working his crossword. "Count on it."

He shrugged and reached for the register. "And it'll be right here, waiting for you."

Back at the garage we were being attacked by strokers. You know the type: tight-fisted bastards with doubt in their eyes. My boss hung the sign out front—oil change and a 21-point inspection for $19.99. We all knew what these days would bring. Tons of tickets with no real money in it. Dale, the owner, would get people with a cheap bargain. And then we'd try to find something else wrong, try to stick it to them. And it worked. Most pulled up with rusted-out exhaust pipes or engines knocking away like busted clocks. But the folks we drew with these deals could barely afford five quarts of 5W-30. So, time and again, they'd simply tell us to *pull her around*, and we'd be stuck with a worthless estimate and a waste of time lube job.

Strokers. They were all over the place today.

Bill was lifting up a giant F-150 that looked about two miles away from the landfill. After catching sight of me, he raised a hand and asked, "How'd it go, Carl?"

But I ignored him. Bill was the only guy I could stand in the shop, but he was a piss-poor mechanic, always scoring weed for the service writer to get better tickets: lightweight brake work that paid two hours for one of actual labor. Plus, all his jobs returned a week later, usually on his day off, so I was the one facing angry people wanting a free fix. Can't blame him though. To make money in this job you had to learn shortcuts. It was no wonder nobody trusted us.

Of course today all I had was a list of oil changes, work we usually left to part-timers. There was nothing big to get my hands into, which was probably good since the thought of my dad's gun under glass, waiting to be sold, was enough to send me into stupid mistakes under the hood. But I couldn't even lift a single car before the boss was already over my shoulder.

"Help you with something, Dale?"

"You're late again, Carl. Now we're really backed up."

The store was Dale's baby, so he came in every day to pry. Even installed cameras in the garage, saying it was for insurance purposes, but we knew he'd sit at home and watch us, just hoping to see something suspicious. Though I suppose I owed the guy. Two priors and a suspended sentence didn't say much for me. Still, a good mechanic was a good mechanic.

"Need you to come in tomorrow," he said, tapping on his clipboard. "Get caught up."

"On Christmas Eve? I still have to get gifts for my family."

"Come in or don't come in." Dale shrugged. "You know what happens if you don't."

I didn't bother arguing, but I also couldn't resist singing "*We wish you a merry Christmas*" until the hoist made enough clatter that all he could do was walk away.

It was freezing in the shop, every tool cold to the touch. As dark approached, the rush quietly came to an end. Bill strolled up to my bay, saying goodnight and sorry about tomorrow.

"Need anything from me?"

I wasn't sure if he was talking drugs or something that would actually help.

"Sheriff Sawyer is coming over tonight. Talk about the case."

The word "sheriff" made Bill sheepish, so he gave me a *happy holidays* and slipped out the back. Dale was in his office, checking time sheets. Usually I'd pop in to say bye, but tonight I left without so much as a sound—though I wasn't in any rush to get home.

Sadie would have a fit about tomorrow, even if it was only a half-day. She hated my hours, my small paychecks, thought I should demand a raise that'd never come. Last night I even heard her tell Geoff that Santa sometimes can't find time for even the best-behaved boys. I wanted to smack her for saying such things. Or maybe just pack up and go for good. Ever since I was a kid, I'd wanted to get out of Iowa, simply waiting to earn enough money to leave and never look back. But then came Geoff. And with him, a wedding and a nice house in Bridger.

Until the factory layoffs. Then jobs were scarce and money was tight, making it impossible to afford a mortgage—property taxes rising so high only rich people could live there now. We were a week from being homeless, which felt like a sign—one last chance to start over somewhere else—until my Grandma Greta died, leaving me a house in Dexton: paid off and move-in ready.

But now, with the lawsuit, even this seemed at risk. Like the more plans I made, the more I was forced to stay. So last night I pulled out the gun case, figuring it was time. They were cursed anyway. One my dad's undoing, the other already leading me into the same kind of trouble.

Except today, with that squad car sitting in my driveway, it felt a bit helpless to know the guns weren't there. As if their sudden absence had left us wide open to any kind of danger.

Geoff was watching TV, some show about the X Games. He was obsessed with bikes and had no idea the day after tomorrow he'd be riding one of his own: a BMX we saw at the mall.

The other half of the five hundred would be Sadie's, though I wasn't sure what to get her. She'd have been happy enough with court fees paid in full, but that didn't seem to be enough this year.

"Hi, buddy. Where's Mom?"

Geoff didn't look away from the screen, watching a kid in baggy pants fly off a dirt ramp. He pointed to the kitchen, where I heard my wife raise her voice: "Those kids are full of it."

"Were you there?" a man said. "Are there any reliable witnesses?"

"Are you calling those punks reliable? They harass the entire neighborhood."

"They're only twelve, Mrs. Dunbar."

"Twelve going on twenty-one," I said, walking into my kitchen. Sadie, still in her diner uniform, sat across the table from a middle-aged cop. The sheriff stood to shake my hand. But despite what he had told me—about how he served with my dad and felt obliged to help—I didn't like his questions. Too many created loopholes. You had to keep the story simple. So I ignored his handshake and said, "They'd obviously been drinking. Police report can verify it."

"That's a different issue, Carl. Assault with a deadly weapon is your concern."

"It was a golf club, Heath. Nothing deadly about that."

"Most people refer to me as Sheriff," the cop said, pointing to his files. "And the report mentions a gun. That two shots were fired."

"So they lied to you," my wife said. "Isn't that enough to get it dismissed?"

"Absolutely." Sawyer stared at his paperwork. "If you can prove it."

"Isn't that your job?" I said, collapsing in a chair. "Sheriff."

"My job is to make sure that boy in there doesn't grow up without a father. And even if you manage to stay out of jail,

I've seen enough kids taken away from parents to last a life-time."

"But that's what *they* are. Just a bunch of kids. And it's my word against theirs."

The sheriff flipped the pages of the report and said exactly what I'd been dreading. "To be honest, Carl, with your record, you'll need more than that."

"That was a year ago. And the charges were dropped. Self-defense. Just like now."

I looked to Sadie for solidarity, but she gazed at her hands as if they held the answer.

"That's a hard thing to prove," Sawyer said. "Without witnesses."

"My wife was at home that night. She could testify."

The cop smiled, as if this was the evidence he'd been hoping for. Instead, Sadie folded her fingers together and quietly said, "I was asleep."

"Asleep, huh?" I stared at her in that little tight dress, cut high above the knee. "Must've been tired working for those tips all day. Guys pay just to watch her pour. Don't they, honey?"

She didn't speak but turned bright red, her skin suddenly the same color as her hair.

Sawyer waved his hands like an umpire calling someone safe at the plate. "Listen, what you need is a lawyer. And maybe a character witness. Do you have anyone to vouch for you?"

But each of us simply avoided the other's eyes, opening up a silence that said it all.

During dinner, Geoff told us about his day at school. Holiday assemblies and eating sweets until his stomach hurt. He didn't even look at his chicken nuggets tonight, but I couldn't blame him. As they say, every good boy deserves a day full of fudge once in a while.

"What are you doing tomorrow?" I asked, a way of slowly getting to the point.

Geoff shrugged, my eight-year-old looking so sad I could hardly stand it.

We didn't let him go out much, the neighborhood too shady for a kid to make even the smallest of snow angels. Foreclosed homes riddled our street, those dark porches lining up like a row of busted piano keys. Vacant lots full of trash littered the entire block. When we moved last fall, my son had to switch school districts, but even Dexton Elementary was full of too many troublemakers to be friends with, which was probably why my boy was so lonely and set apart.

When I was little, even if there was nothing to do, we could at least stay out past sunset. But now it was as if that world, like all childhood memories, had become a thing of the past.

I took a sip of beer. "Maybe Mom can keep you company."

My wife dropped her fork to the plate with a sharp crack. "And where will you be, Carl?"

"Earning overtime. You know, keeping myself out of trouble."

Geoff moved his nuggets around, considering a bite.

"Great," Sadie said. "Maybe on Christmas you can send us a card?"

Blood burned through my body, but I took a deep breath, tried to stay focused on my son.

"Tomorrow night we'll go look at the lights." It was a silly thing to say, knowing that the only decorations strung up around here were at the cop shop, the one place nobody bothered them.

"Okay," Geoff mumbled, knowing the same things we did about our street.

"Why do you do that?" Sadie walked to the sink and ran water.

"What did I do?" I asked, though by the way her body shook it was clear she was fighting tears. I gave Geoff a shrug, tussled his hair. When he didn't look at me, I lifted his chin and gave him a wink. But all I got in return was an empty face, those big eyes blankly gazing back.

While Geoff watched TV, the Christmas specials coming one after another, I snuck up behind Sadie washing the dishes, buried my face in her red hair.

"What happened at work?" she asked.

I pressed myself against her and said, "You know Dale. He has me on a short leash."

"You keep giving him an excuse to." She stared down at the greasy suds. Streaks of flour ran along the nape of her neck. "You think he'd help us? Testify on your behalf?"

"He's not the best character himself."

My hands wandered around her waist, figuring it was one way to end a fight. But when I lifted her skirt, she moved away, told me to stop.

"What's your problem, Sadie?"

"That all your problems become my problems."

She scrubbed at the dark stains I'd left on her dress. No matter how many times I washed them, my hands never seemed to get fully clean. As if the oil had forever soaked into the skin, making everything they touched turn to black.

"We wouldn't have a problem if you'd have my back for once."

"Every time I think things are different, you always end up—" She shook her head and threw the dish rag at me. "Clean up your own mess for once. And if this goes to court..."

I wondered what she'd say would happen next: prison? divorce? bankruptcy?

Instead, my wife simply shook her head and whispered, "Golf clubs." Then she sighed and walked from the room, leaving me with nothing but a sink full of dirty dishes.

***

151

Last spring, for our anniversary, we actually got a babysitter
for once, just so I could treat Sadie to dinner. Afterward, we
stopped for a drink, the night settling around my talk about
the future, those plans I still had in mind. My wife listened,
even acted like she believed it, making me wonder why I made
it so hard on her sometimes. It's also maybe why, at last call,
when she went to order one final round and a stranger at the
bar laid his own money down instead, I felt that awful animal growing inside me again. Sadie waved the guy away, but
he kept floating back to flirt until, finally, his hand fell upon
hers, and my head rushed with thoughts that often came in
those moments when the world tilted off its axis: images of
Sadie happier with another man, the sort who paid for drinks
and held her hand.

I don't remember much about it. When the cops arrived,
I swore to them I tried to talk it out. That everything was
all under control until the guy kept insisting he didn't mean
anything by it. But one thing I can't stand is a liar. So when
the pushing and punching began, there was little choice in
how to end it. And with only a beer bottle nearby, it was
either me or him. Except the cops still took us both: me to jail,
him to the hospital. There wasn't even a need for stitches, so
the guy dropped the charges, probably embarrassed for being
bested in a bar brawl. I pictured him later showing off the
scar like some kind of trophy, while I had to be picked up the
next morning by my wife and child. Geoff wore pajamas. Both
of them looked half-asleep. And though my boy was worried
about the bruises and black eye, wanted to kiss them better
like his mama had always taught him, Sadie said to not touch
me. That it wouldn't do any good this time.

This evening, Geoff's stomach still bothered him, so he went
to bed without protest. It amazed me what a fine boy we'd
somehow raised. In fact, it often made Sadie want to try for

another. But no matter how hard I worked, we never seemed to get far enough ahead to afford it. And whenever Sadie dreamt out loud about going to night school, trying for a better job, I stumbled into that same old shame, like maybe some men inherit a life that just can't be made square.

So, before bed, though Sadie complained about a headache and being bone-tired, she didn't put up too much of a fight when I pushed her on the mattress and climbed on top. At first, she avoided my mouth, told me *not tonight*, but when I gave her hair a tug and worked myself between her legs, it was like every other time our bodies met. Fast at the start, with Sadie lying stock-still and acting like she wanted to get it over with. But soon things slowed and sighs turned to whispers, words going back and forth about God, about love. I never know if they're true or if the things we say in those moments are only of the moment. We certainly don't tell them by light of day. But in the dark, it's as if we're strangers, allowing us to remember who we once were. And afterward, in those seconds before sleep arrives, between catching our breath and closing our eyes, I can almost sense those old forgotten selves, lingering there, just below the surface.

I awoke to gunshots, the edge of a scream clenched between my teeth. I waited for another shot, but the sounds were simply an echo from the same tired dream. In it, my dad's voice came and went, talking nonsense about living right and dying wrong. Of course, I knew they were words of my own making—all the things I wished he'd said. Though who in their right mind would listen to someone that had it all backwards from the beginning? In the dream, I sometimes asked him why he did it, what was so tough about sticking it out, how maybe things would've been different if he had. But my dad's only answer was to pick up that gun, again and again.

***

It was still dark when I stepped outside. Usually Sadie would be at work by now, serving that overlap between first and third shift, while I drove our son to school. But this morning, the house was asleep, and it was snowing. So I let the truck idle a bit, trying to warm up. And though the trees on our block were already dead, bare branches clacking like bones in the wind, at this hour, with those flakes drifting down, turning everything white, the place looked almost peaceful.

At work, it felt nice to be alone. It'd be a slow shift, nothing one man couldn't handle. Even strokers took a day off. But as I put a car on the lift, ready to pull its transmission—a job that may actually pay since it'd take all morning just to get the thing out—the front doorbell buzzed. Its echo ricocheted through the garage, making my wrench slip. Maybe I was still shaky from last night, images of lawyers and lost little boys sitting in my mind. But it didn't help when I entered the waiting room and saw one of the kids from the lawsuit, a small woman at his side.

"What are you doing here?" I was in no mood for the talk that was about to happen.

The lady looked like she hadn't slept, eyes puffed out at the edges. She wore a threadbare coat. Dirty slippers covered her feet. "My son has something to say to you."

The boy appeared hungover. In fact, with the mom gripping his arm, he looked like any average teenager: sullen and shy. Nothing like the other night when I stepped out onto my porch and told him and his friends to get off my property. In the dark all I saw were white-trash kids wearing sweatshirts with huge hoods, those low-slung jeans and stocking caps hung at an angle. And when they approached my truck, holding something shiny—a slim jim? maybe a crowbar?—it was enough in my eyes to protect my home by any means necessary.

"It's nothing he can't tell me in a courtroom, lady."

"We're here to say sorry." She let go of the boy and crossed her arms.

None of us moved, and I had to wonder if this was where we'd wind up someday: my son wearing sloppy shoes and saggy pajama pants; Sadie wrapped up in thin clothes and seeming so much older than herself. The thought alone made me yearn for work, to walk back into the shop and earn that extra pay so we could get the hell away from these people.

"I don't hear an apology."

She gave him a nudge and the boy mumbled a quick sorry.

"My son doesn't need any more strikes against him," she said, pulling the kid back. "And I figure you need a witness to forget what they saw. Or heard. So maybe we can make a deal."

I knew my fair share about being a teenager in trouble, but it felt unfair how some folks never had to pay the price, always looking to cut some deal to worm their way out of it.

"Maybe some kids need to learn a lesson about third strikes—and where it can land you."

I tapped a wrench into my open palm and glanced at the clock.

I still had to go to the mall, buy something for my wife and child. Plus, now, maybe swing by the pawnshop, see if they had a set of golf clubs for sale.

"That's how you want it?" She yanked her son to the door. "You're right about this guy."

"What kind of parent are you?" I asked. "Letting a kid hang out with a bunch of thugs?"

"You want a fight?" she said, wearing a look only a mother could give. "You got one."

Once they left, I thought about tomorrow. How, despite the presents I planned to put under the tree, with just a few words of forgiveness I could've given my wife the one thing she wanted. But now all I had in store for her was another battle, one more war she didn't want to wage.

***

I walked back into the shop, except the thought of putting my arms around that transmission, wrestling it out with a chain, was too much. The morning had made for distraction, a good way to get hurt when you're alone in a garage. At least that's what I told Dale later that night when he called, wondering why the place had closed early, why he was getting complaints all day. But at the moment, with that heat in my stomach burning like an ulcer, I simply had to get out of there.

Snow had piled along the shoulder of the highway, dirty and unable to melt under a gray sky. In Bridger, the outlet mall was full of cars, more folks making a last-ditch effort. Inside, people ran around wearing ties and dresses, making me feel exposed in a grimy shirt—my name embroidered on the front for all to see. The toy store was wall-to-wall moms and dads, shoving money this way and that, trying to get whatever their kids' lists wished for. It was crazy how hard we all tried to make life special, if only for one morning. A brief moment when grown-ups could maybe feel like good parents again. I took the money clip from my pocket, holding it in front of me like some passport that'd gain me access to a little boy's bike.

But when I got to the aisle, it'd been ransacked, each hook completely empty.

I grabbed a clerk running through the horde and said, "You had a bike. A BMX on sale."

He looked at me as if I was a savage, something dangerous and lost in time.

"Sir, we've been out of those for days."

"But it was here. Not long ago."

The kid removed my hand from his arm. "It's the day before Christmas."

"I know that." I gritted my teeth and held my stack of money to his face. "But maybe you have one in back. Something you've been setting aside."

The clerk smirked as if bribes were common around here, and I saw myself through his eyes: another stroker looking for a deal. "Sir, I can put it on backorder. That's the best I can do."

Before I could say more, he was pulled away by someone else. Sweat rolled down my face, the money wet in my hands. I wandered through the store, looking for something any kid would want. There were all kinds of plastic creatures with missiles attached to their arms, swords jutting from fists—violent things I refused to put in the hands of my son. I didn't even know how to pronounce the names of half of these objects. So when I saw the sleds, a dozen untouched discs hanging from the wall, I grabbed two and headed for the register.

I wasn't sure what to get Sadie. I walked into the lingerie store, but it felt too sexy for Christmas. I browsed jewelry but, despite all the shiny stones, nothing spoke to me of my wife. She always said she didn't need that kind of stuff. Plus, if I got a diamond necklace or a fancy bracelet, the fact that she'd have one precious piece sitting there by itself in a box felt even more pathetic. Especially when I couldn't even get my own son something as simple as a bike.

The air in each store was dry and hot and I couldn't take the crowd anymore, but in my truck, I felt turned around, driving without direction. Times like these, unsettled and misplaced, I often visited the cemetery at the edge of town. Geoff always wanted to come along, but I didn't want him to read the lie my grandparents put on my dad's tombstone—*Good Husband, Generous Father*—or see the shortened dates between those parentheses. It seemed wrong to introduce him to that legacy at such a young age. Plus, he'd have questions, and I'd never have answers. In fact, whenever I stood over his grave, the only thing I ever saw was a man's breaking point—and a family he clearly didn't want. But today it almost made sense. How someone could feel they were doing the world a favor, offering it a gift by simply removing themselves from it.

Now, with my head burning with such notions, I drove in circles—until finally pulling up to the pawnshop. It was locked for the holiday, so I had to cup my hands to peer into the dark windows, hoping to find a sign of life. It was probably another common scene, a man begging for something he'd left behind. But when a shadow started to move about inside, I knocked until the glass almost cracked in its frame. And soon enough, there stood the broker behind his metal bars, holding a rifle and saying, "Get out of here before I call the cops."

"I want to buy back my gun. Then I'll leave."

He took a labored breath. "I suggest you back up and get the hell out of here."

I held out the cash, the same roll of bills he'd given me the day before.

"I only want the one. And then I'll leave."

"Are you kidding?" The guy nearly grinned. "You think I'd sell to someone like *you*?"

When he pulled the bolt with a soft click, I knew my dad's gun was gone and out of my hands for good. And though I felt hollowed out, staring at that locked door like a kid kicked out of class, there was also an ease about the emptiness. Some strange sigh of relief that couldn't be completely denied as I walked away—trying my hardest to not look back.

As I entered the house, Sadie was in the kitchen trying to set-tle someone down. I only caught a trace of the phone conver-sation, but it was pretty clear who was on the other end. Dale would forgive me, always did. Sadie, on the other hand, was probably thinking the worst, never giving me the benefit of the doubt. What was the point of a lawyer when my own wife thought I deserved everything I had coming? Still, it didn't seem fair that she got to be in charge of how my life worked. That she had the final say on things. So when I saw Geoff on the floor, watching his X Games, I snuck up behind and whispered, "Want an early present?"

The boy's eyes perked up as he bounded from the floor into my arms. I led him to my truck and unveiled the sleds. He stared at the plastic as if it was about to bite. And there was no denying the disappointment in his voice when he said, "I like them."

"Should we try it out?"

When he nodded, I put him in the cab and swung out of the driveway.

I had no idea where we were headed, but part of me thought it was finally time to go for good, just take off with my boy to a land outside of Iowa.

But we'd barely left our own street when Geoff asked, "Isn't Mom coming?"

"Not today. It's just you and me now. Right?"

"I guess," he said, smiling. But it was easy to hear the tremble behind the words.

"What? Don't you want some guy time with Dad?"

Geoff shrugged. "It just feels like this is something a family should do."

"You've been watching too much TV."

Instead of a laugh, he scooted away to stare out the window. And though I didn't want to look, it was impossible not to see his reflection in the glass, those empty eyes slowly filling up.

By now, Sadie was probably in a panic. I imagined her calling the cops, describing the situation in her own way. And how when all was said and done, she'd always end up the saint: *Loving Mother; Put-upon Wife.* Just another good woman abandoned by a do-nothing man.

Because, soon enough, everything catches up to everyone, leading to another strike that'd finally take me where I'd been headed all along—for a long stretch, depending on the judge.

And no deal would help me worm out of it this time.

So, today, when I saw the one slope that passed for a hill on our block, it felt like a last chance to give my boy a parting gift as I hit the brake and said, "This looks like the spot."

It was just a vacant lot, so often choked with trash you couldn't even see the drop. But today, snow covered the garbage, revealing a small decline, pretty as a painting.

The flakes were about to fall again and the dark was coming on fast, so I tucked the sleds under my arm and led Geoff to the edge. My son surveyed the scene, as if plotting out the course, until he looked up to me as if asking for a bit of advice, something to get him through this new terrain.

"I want you to remember this day. Will you do that for me?" But before he could say yes or no, I pushed a disc into his hands. It looked huge next to his small body. We dropped the sleds side-by-side. Then I picked up my boy and plopped him onto the plastic, saying, "Hold on tight."

"Are you sure this is okay?" he said with a thread of worry. The kid knew as well as anyone that this wasn't any kind of place to fool around. I mean, who knew what kind of sharp-edged objects lay beneath all that white stuff.

"Who's going to stop us?" I said, crouching down behind him. "Ready to launch?"

"Wait. Aren't you coming too?"

I put my palms against his back, ready to shove my son down into that hole, but not before giving him a promise that I'd be right there when he hit bottom.

SEPARATE, BODIES

REASONS

It was a few hours after she got the news of her dad's death, while attending a house party, that Hannah first met her next boyfriend. It'd rained all night and the whole city felt soggy underfoot. So when she showed up soaking wet, hair frizzed, he introduced himself by saying he preferred women without makeup. And she liked that he was a grad student in philosophy, someone close to her age who liked girls with curves and piercings, everything about her slick rubber rain boots and how they shined. That night he called himself Tom, and it was only weeks later, searching through his wallet while he slept, that Hannah discovered he spelled it, mysteriously, with an *h*.

Thom. A name fit for a boy who wore jeans low on his hip, a bit skinny in the leg.

But it all started at that party, when she couldn't stop looking at him looking at her.

Sure, he had a nice bend to his nose. And yes, there was the way his cheekbones lifted high from his face. But it was also how he spoke. When asked at some point in the shifting small talk about wanting children, he said strange things like, "Babies? I think I've heard of those." And it was also how he chose not to speak. Like when he listened to music and didn't say a word, letting the drugs run their course, a grin dangling from his lips.

So that first night it'd been quick and without question, her fingers running down each knob of his spine, his hands filled with her hair. She etched the outline of his twisting tattoos with a shy finger. It tickled when he sucked on the stud in her tongue. And then there was the way his eyes roved her face as if looking for something beneath.

All these things were the reasons, of course. How could they not be? But lately Hannah wondered whether reasons were always the best basis to make decisions upon.

THE ACT OF EATING

Day twenty-one of the heat wave in Iowa City and they were still together. Outside, everything was green and sticky, rain coming sometimes twice a day. This morning they stayed in bed, wet sheets piled on the floor, legs sprawled across each other. It was Sunday and Hannah wanted to go job-searching. Summer classes were just starting, but the loans were already running out.

"I didn't realize you were the job type?" Thom said, words sliding from his mouth. The first thing he did after waking up was roll a joint. The conversations sometimes took forever. He snuggled next to her, both of them still sweating. "It's so provincial it's almost cute."

Hannah wasn't sure whether to be flattered or insulted; everything they spoke of seemed so slippery in that way. "Since when is it cute to be able to eat?"

Thom closed his eyes. "Since when hasn't it?"

She nearly fell back to sleep, but instead took a shower and got dressed. When she left, he was standing in the kitchen eating dry toast without a shirt on. His skin looked thin, like a paper bag holding all those bones. And watching him take tiny bird-bites, it seemed somehow true. She rarely did see him eat. In fact, watching him choke down a slice of bread, the sight felt almost sad, like watching a bodybuilder take a nap or a movie star clip his nails. It was hard to believe somebody like Thom ever sneezed, or peed, or did anything like anybody else.

JOB SEARCH

The job search was futile to the point of funny. At first, she applied for positions in offices, air-conditioned and quiet. Something along the lines of reception or administrative assistant, those hand-me-down titles that boiled down to making coffee or copies. Instead, each application listed a set of tasks she could barely translate. And when certain sections asked for *Degrees or Certifications*, Hannah had to face up to the fact that at twenty-nine she still had neither.

There was always waitressing or retail, things she'd had her hand in for years, until Hannah came upon a store selling crucifixes. Through the window, their metal caught the light, as if to appear truly holy. She'd never been to church but could imagine the smell of pews and Pine-Sol, voices murmuring a quick "Peace be with you." In the display, some crosses were small and simple, others large and ornate, but all of them felt sacred in a way she'd never experienced on Sunday mornings. Hannah wanted to cry at the sight, but couldn't. Instead, she walked in, bought a cheap necklace, and asked for an application.

SMALL BAPTISMS

Thom found it hilarious, of course. That evening before going to bed, he stared at the thin crucifix around her neck and shook his head. The cross was close to invisible but still bright.

"That's perfect, Hannah. Does it make you feel like a virgin?"

She giggled because, in a way, it did. And that night, while she sat atop him, Hannah noticed a newfound adoration. His fingers kept moving toward the little piece of gold between her breasts. His gaze never lifted from her eyes. And it made Hannah wonder if falling in love was always this easy, like being born again, and again, and again.

CONCENTRIC PATTERNS

Hannah's mother never talked about her dad, except to call him a mistake. So several years ago, when he briefly came back into their lives, when her mom's last words focused on forgiving and forgetting, Hannah just rolled her eyes and walked away. Figured it was the morphine talking. So it was no surprise when, after her funeral, the guy acted like a parent for about five minutes before vanishing as well. But what *did* surprise Hannah was how his sudden absence seemed to entirely replace her mom's—as if a new death had somehow arrived without warning. Call it a mother's legacy, or a father's curse, but for a long time afterward, Hannah felt like she was living outside her own body: a small shadow moving from place to place, person to person.

Now it was almost hard to recall that blur of years, until twenty-one days ago, when the police called to ask if she was the next of kin. Then, as she took in the details—a motorcycle, a crash, a backroad near the border—it was as if the world had spun back on a loop. Yet, it also felt like eavesdropping on the story of some stranger's life, forcing Hannah to simply listen from the audience, curious how it would all end—unsure where the plot could possibly go from here.

Weeks later, in bed with Thom, she wondered what her mom would've thought about it. But, of course, Hannah never really knew the woman well enough to know what she'd say about anything. So, instead, she asked the boy next to her, curious for his thoughts on life after death.

"You think some part of us still sticks around? You know, just in case?"

At first Thom said nothing, stoned and staring off into the

void. Hannah always wanted to know where he went when he seemed so far away. Her fingers stroked his bare chest, tracing the corkscrew nature of the tattoos. She liked that he had no hair anywhere. Like a newborn baby of a man. It made her want to kiss him everywhere.

Then, as she began to nod off in the heat, a voice echoed into her ear. "Sometimes saying goodbye is the best kind of hello."

It was like being sung a song, encouraging on the outside but still derisive at its center. And though the words were somewhat cryptic, maybe even a little rehearsed, it was exactly what Hannah needed to hear: things that sounded hopeful in one way, half hostile in another.

Q AND A

One day after her gross anatomy class—a course she registered for with the hope that science had better answers than all her other attempted majors—the professor called out to her from down the hall. He slid up alongside and matched her gait, catching his breath. "Got to stop smoking."

"You run an anatomy lab and still smoke?"

"Just started." He grinned and shrugged. "Seemed too early to quit."

It was a nice comment, but lately she was wary of witty remarks. "Is there a problem?"

"What a great question." The man—though he seemed too young to call him that—smiled some more. "Isn't that a great question?"

She wasn't sure whether to listen or leave. "Do you always reply to questions with a question?"

"Do you?" He slapped his forehead. "There I go again."

Hannah could only manage a small smirk. She was going to be late for work. Then later Thom was taking her out again to watch another band looking for a break.

"Sorry," he said. "I just noticed you were new to the program."

"My advisor told me to take your class this summer. Get it out of the way."

"Out of the way of what?"

"Before fall comes." Hannah felt her face turn red. "He said it was a weed-out course."

"I see," he said, holding out his hand. Hannah had to admit the wedding ring disappointed her a bit. "Well, I just wanted to say it's really nice to see a fresh face in class."

"That's kind of you, Professor Davis, but—"

"Ben. My name is Ben." He took her hand but didn't shake it. "It's good to meet you..."

"My boyfriend calls me Hannah." His fingers went limp in hers. "Anyway, it's kind of you to say, Professor Davis. But I'm pretty sure I'm the oldest student in class. By a few years."

"I know," he said, putting his other hand on top of theirs. "That's what makes it nice."

UNSEEN DEVOTIONS

Maude wore coal-colored stoles each day, as if taking a life-long penance. She was old to be sure, but to think of her as grandmotherly would've been a mistake. Hannah made the error early on when telling the new boss *she* would take the box of Bible pamphlets to the backroom. That *she'd* stay late while they locked up. Don't be silly, of course she'd walk her home at night.

Maude took the politeness for a while until finally saying, "Honey, will you please shush up about it already?"

One afternoon Hannah was dusting countertops, trying to look busy, when Maude asked her if she had the spirit. It was a long-awaited question. Hannah had expected it during her interview. But religion was rarely mentioned in the store except when Maude held her weekly prayer groups in the storeroom. "I thought you'd never ask."

Maude didn't flinch.

"My mother said religion was like any other racket. Lots

of fake rules and false promises. So people end up wasting their entire lives sweating over some test that can never be passed."

"Not in this life," Maude whispered, her voice turning raspy like a ghost. "That reward comes after the test. But the question, dear, is what are you studying right now?"

She wasn't sure what to tell the old woman. Last spring, due to several semesters of erratic enrollment, Hannah had been relegated to a General Studies major, which was often humiliating to admit. Sometimes she'd brag about being a Renaissance woman, learning a bit of everything. At quieter moments, though, it felt like she was being taught to be neither here nor there.

"I guess I'm still trying to figure that out."

"Good," Maude said. "That's a good girl."

That evening, while Hannah polished crucifixes, people entered the store one by one and silently went to the backroom. Some were elderly like Maude, while others were younger than expected, but all were women who looked so heartbroken it was hard to even ask *How may I help you?* As the prayer session took place, Hannah tried not to pry, except the store never had many customers, much less on a Wednesday night. So she soon found herself in the back hall, ear pressed against the storeroom, curious about what happens behind such closed doors.

BODY ART

Thom loved to take Hannah to concerts in town, her skin taking on the smell of bars and beer. Tonight the place was packed, bodies abuzz with the last set: a hardcore screamer of a band who played without pause. Her ears rang, radiating small shivers into her jaw. She knew in the morning her hair would stink of cigarette smoke, a scent that couldn't be shampooed away.

Thom pulled her close. She felt the prod of his pelvis as he said, "They were okay."

Like most nights, while they waited for the next act—a reggae group full of white boys—a young man with spiky hair approached Thom, asking, "Hey, you interested in joining a band?"

Thom had the look of knowing each song before it was sung though he didn't know how to play a note. So, as always, he offered the same reply: "I don't believe in rock stars."

It sounded like the truth. The only honest thing worth believing amongst these people, who despite the individual genre they fit into—hipster, emo, punk—all appeared to be a part of the same organism. Everyone looked like they made their own clothes. Each of them had thick plastic shards gaping their earlobes. The man standing to her left had asterisks circling his neck—tattoos a form of speech between Thom's friends; a way to code one another.

And though part of Hannah also had the desire to color herself separate, bodies struggling for distinction, another part of her felt embarrassed for them. How each looked so alike by trying to look so different. But when she turned to share this with Thom, he was no longer there. And when she felt the click of the metal barbell against her own teeth, Hannah was curious which version of the truth she belonged to.

LONELIER OF THE TWO

The next time they met in class, Ben ignored her as she went from one dead cat to the next, pins jutting out of each organ like small flags at a cemetery. Hannah wondered what these body parts looked like inside of her. Possibly bigger than a feline's. Maybe more pink, filled with blood, everything operating together without her knowledge. There was a beauty in it, a fragile perfection in how life worked, but it was difficult to be inspired with all these sliced-open animals sprawled on metal tables. So she took notes, listing off the terms that'd be on the test.

After class, once all the students had left, she stood by Ben's desk, not sure what she was doing until he told her to take a seat.

She sat down on a nearby stool and asked, "How can you stand the smell in here?"

Ben shrugged. "You get used to it."

"I don't know if I could. To be around bodies all day. Maybe I'm not cut out for this."

"I wanted to be a surgeon." Ben lifted his shoulders again. He was full of shrugs today. "But now I'm more of a librarian, labeling organs and helping people find what they need."

"Shouldn't a TA run the lab? Give you time to cure an important disease or something?"

"All new faculty have to earn their stripes. I just moved here this year. From back East."

"So what made you want to do this?"

"Another great question. At first, it was to be closer to family. But now, I'm not so sure."

"No, I mean why bio-chemistry? It even sounds depressing." She crossed her legs and pointed to the room full of dead cats. "Lonely, if nothing else."

"It is, sometimes," he said, fiddling with his wedding ring. "But really it's the living who are the real pain in the cadaver." He laughed at his own punchline—if it even was one—then picked up a beaker of clear fluid, took a drink, and gagged. His hands clasped his throat. Hannah knocked over her stool, unsure of how to help, until he giggled. "Just kidding. It's only water."

Something about Ben was like a younger brother: inexplicably annoying yet lovable. Other times, he reminded Hannah of husbands on TV, telling their dad jokes and trying so hard to get his kids to like him. Either way, it was nice to be around someone and not feel some kind of pressure to perform. She picked up the stool and placed it as close to his as she could.

"Actually, it's the opposite." Ben grabbed a graduated cylinder, filled it with water, and handed it over. "Trying to fix

169

people who are in constant need. That's the lonelier of the two."

Hannah thought about her mom. How near the end, she needed so little, and her daughter had refused to give even that much. Not to mention the coroner, who kept calling every day, curious what to do with her dad's ashes. "I don't know. Dead people can be pretty demanding."

"You'd think so," he said, "but the dead don't require any-thing from us. Not anymore."

Hannah heard the tears in his voice. But when she tried to ask more about it, Ben held a finger to his lips and gently tapped his glass to hers, offering a small chime to the conver-sation.

THE DEPARTED

Thom on top of her, inside of her, his hands framing her face, while her mind drifted back to her mother. Hannah was sick with herself, lifeless, not there at all. She tried to remain utterly still, silent—cold despite the heat. She barely even breathed. But when Thom finished, smoking his pipe and not speaking a word of worry about it, Hannah wondered if he knew the difference between the living and the dead. If he even under-stood what it felt like to touch the thing that makes one seem so alive one minute and completely departed the next.

SUMMER SLUMP

The day had been slow. There was a new shipment of inspi-rational CDs to display, murky sounds of ocean currents and seagulls. Craft supplies arrived with cutouts of halos so kids could wear their own crowns. With the heat gaining outside, people often stumbled into the shadowy store to escape the sun. But most were browsers, picking up candles and prayer cards, cracking a couple grins to her behind the counter before slowly making their way toward the door.

"Summer," Maude said as the bell tolled above the exit.

"Nothing doing until Advent."

It was Christmas in July. Hannah stocked snow globes and wreathed the room in laurel.

In a few weeks, she'd turn thirty, making the idea of decorations during a drought feel more like wishful thinking. In fact, Hannah wondered if she'd still even be here by December.

"I imagine that would be a busy time of year."

"Christmas isn't just a day on the calendar."

"Maybe. To me it feels like any other birthday. Lots of build-up followed by a bunch of letdowns." She could almost hear her mom's voice, as if she'd been suddenly possessed.

But even if it was meant to be funny, Maude held out her arms and said, "I'm so sorry."

Hannah clenched against the embrace like a snared animal. Recently, everyone felt the need to hold her, as if she always seemed cold. And though the hug was bony and Maude smelled like damp paper, something about it made her ask, "What do you do in the back?"

"I thought you'd never ask," the old woman said, her breath warm against Hannah's ear.

THE DIFFERENCE

Thom refused to meet her at work. The very idea of walking into the place made him sneer, though Hannah knew it actually made him nervous. Every time they talked about Maude, the store, the crosses hanging from the ceiling like fly-traps, Thom's skin went slick, his eyes darting about the room. Though at first it annoyed her, this reaction now gave her the strangest of joys.

After work, they met down the street at a record store. Thom sat at a counter with the store's owner, nodding along to the latest demo from some local folk singer. Hannah wasn't sure how he spent his time. Thom didn't attend class, yet earned the grades he needed to stick around. The very idea of graduation sent him into diatribes that weren't fully serious or entirely silly.

Now, with the last notes still in the air, he opened his eyes as if noticing her for the first time.

"There she is," he said. "Back from the holy land."

The man behind the counter dug in his register. Then Thom suddenly spoke as if he'd been asked a question. "You don't have to be a musician, but you have to be an artist."

"What's the difference?" Hannah asked.

He smirked. "What do you think the difference is?"

Hannah wanted to say she didn't think it meant anything. That it was just a bunch of words. But instead she hid her hands in her pockets and said she didn't know.

"It means this songwriter doesn't understand anything about life."

It felt brilliant. It sounded unquestionable. But it was bizarre how certain truths could often seem so absurd, so utterly irrelevant. "And you do?"

The owner chuckled without looking up from his drawer.

"Hannah, Hannah, Hannah." Thom walked behind and rubbed her shoulders.

"Thom, Thom, Thom."

He gently gripped the back of her neck. "My work is *in* the field of life."

She felt like she'd heard the phrase before. "What does that mean?"

"Yeah, Thom. What does that mean?" The owner leaned against the counter, winking.

"What do you mean what does it mean?"

"Can't you give a straight answer?" she asked, freeing herself from his hold.

The boy stood frozen, his fingers hanging in the air, looking like they wanted to choke her. "If you don't know, Hannah, it's certainly not my job to tell you."

"Hallelujah to that," she yelled, raising her hand high as if waiting to be called upon.

FINAL EXAMINATIONS

Hannah strolled from one cadaver to the next, writing specific organs on the appropriate line.

The tests were taken individually. Everyone else sat outside in the hall, rummaging through notes and waiting for a turn to walk the maze of human bodies, which lay open on the tables, their skin pinned back with thick needles, like strangers waiting to be named—people she felt responsible for making whole again if only by identifying their independent parts.

Hannah was staring at someone's liver when she felt a sudden presence enter her space.

She tried to focus on the next question, the next answer, but her hands trembled. The handwriting took on an unreadable slant. The air lit up, electrified with watching eyes. She pictured phantoms above her, looking over her shoulder and shaking their heads, until finally she sensed breath on the back of her neck. It was hot and smelled like smoke. Hannah didn't want to turn, didn't want to see the source. The hovering was enough for her to feel less alone, less alive, until she recognized the voice of the man who worked with the dead for a living.

"You sure that's correct?" Ben's hand grazed her hip as he reached for the pen.

It wasn't like she imagined. She thought the first touch would be tender. That it'd feel like a blessing upon her body. Instead, his fingers were clammy. He leaned into her back. His mouth next to her ear sounded wet as it whispered, "Let me help you."

He guided her pen, scratching out *bile* duct and replacing it with *cystic*.

His hands then slid around her ribcage, pressing on her diaphragm.

"This is the gallbladder." The fingers glided down to her stomach. "Bile builds up, drains down, until it finally stops, here, in the small intestine."

She felt each word on her skin. The heat of his breath in the cold lab made her prickle. She wanted to squirm, push him away, but instead let her head drop back against his chest.

"I thought the dead didn't worry about such things."

"They don't get grades either."

"Except isn't this cheating?"

Hannah waited for another one-liner, something juvenile that'd make it all a game again.

But Ben's hands quickly lifted, leaving her body cool in the spots he had kept warm. "I'm sorry. You're right."

He moved across the room as silently as he'd approached, leaving her standing there, feeling flushed and foolish. "What do you think you're doing?"

Ben walked to his desk and attempted one of his smiles, though it sagged at the corners. He looked like a schoolboy caught in the act, which made Hannah feel suddenly like a mother, scolding her son for not knowing better. It was something her own mom did for most of her life, seducing and comforting men like a full-time job, a thankless role she could never quit. Instead, like any good parent, she'd spend the day complaining about her children, only to laugh it off as if it couldn't be helped—a memory that quickly cracked something open inside Hannah as well, starting with a snicker, a small cackle, before the laugh turned into absolute silence, the sound so strong it stuck in her throat and almost came close to crying, making it difficult to tell the difference between the two: the tears seeming at once funny and then again not.

LOST AND FOUND

That night, after the doors were locked and the lights turned out, Hannah stood in the storeroom holding hands. The women wouldn't stop smiling when she entered with Maude wrapped in the crook of her arm. The room was dank. Brick walls sweated with water. The concrete floor felt slippery beneath her shoes. As each member kissed her cheek, first one and then the other, Maude never left her side. Everyone nodded at her as if they saw something she couldn't, as if they'd all been waiting for this moment to arrive. Then they asked about each other's week.

Kathy, a woman with shaky hands, said her condition was receding, praise be to Him.

Ann, a grandma of five, said she welcomed the latest miracle into the world: number six.

Yolanda, a student with the smallest of accents, finally received her financial aid.

Then without word or gesture, as if reading each other's mind, a circle formed—hands clasped, eyes closed, lips silently moving. Hannah tried to follow along, staring at the concentration in their faces, the way the hair hung down around their bowed heads like shawls.

Soon enough, there was a collective sigh. The women looked up as if waking from a sound sleep.

Then the grinning began again—because it was now time to share.

The youngest girl in the circle, a freshman at best, wanted to ask forgiveness for carnal acts. She'd slept with her boyfriend, giving in to his pleas, but now wasn't sure what it meant.

Nobody spoke, either to condemn or approve. Then, after some silence, Maude lifted Hannah's hand in the air and said, "Let's pray for our latest lost lamb who's now been found."

Everyone stared, never stopping their smiles. Hannah's palms were hot despite the cold. And though she was never asked to talk, never allowed a question, she felt a strange need to make a speech, address the group, possibly clear the air. But before she could open her mouth, before she could confess a thing, the circle had slowly closed in. It was like from some grade-school game, the women surrounding her as if she was a nucleus that gravitated group hugs.

There was the fear at first, then an inclination to run, but in the end all Hannah could do was stand there, tightly bracing herself against the swarm.

BLACKOUT

On the street, Hannah couldn't stop sweating even though her body wouldn't stop shaking. She wasn't sure of direction, which way she was headed. Her brain felt full of blood, the throb coming and going. All she remembered was being embraced for what seemed like minutes, hours, days, until she couldn't breathe. But it was only when she began to hyperventilate that all the women let go at once, dropping Hannah so fast she lost her footing on the wet cement.

The last thing she heard was her head hitting the concrete with an audible crack.

When her eyes opened, she was laid out in the front of the store, everything dark as if in a dream. Maude kneeled next to her, wiping her face with a moist rag.

"We were just praying for you. And now here you've come to us again."

Hannah sat up and rubbed the knot on the back of her head. "I have to go."

"Are you sure, honey?" The old woman clutched an arm, her hands stronger than expected as she helped Hannah find her feet. "I mean, we were just getting started."

"I could have a concussion." She didn't know anything about concussions, hadn't even studied them yet, but the need to leave overwhelmed her. "I have to get to a hospital."

"Of course, dear. I'll take you."

Hannah shook herself free from Maude's grasp and stumbled across the store. The old woman kept repeating her name, whispering the word like a question, which almost tempted her to turn around. Until she finally reached the door, unbolting the lock so fast that by the time the raspy voice called out again, asking her to come back, Hannah was already safe on the other side.

SUTURED

Now, wandering the streets, passing store after store, Hannah felt queasy. Her lips were thick with thirst. Her tongue was swollen; it clenched the barbell tight and made her mouth ache. She searched for a drinking fountain, a soda machine, and instead found herself in front of a tattoo parlor.

The door was propped open, letting in the night air. Inside, the walls were filled with cartoons of aliens and calligraphy. And there were crosses, tons of them, in every shape and size.

When she entered, the smell of hot ink made her dizzy. She leaned against the doorframe. The thought of something absorbing into her bloodstream brought on a wave of nausea.

So instead she asked the guy with a two-foot ponytail: "What about piercings?"

The man behind a glass counter gave her a blank stare, as if unsure of the request.

"I have money."

He paused, then motioned her into a small room where she was told to lie down.

She closed her eyes and pointed to her mouth, saying, "Take your time."

There was a squawk of rubber gloves swabbing a needle. "Ready?"

She nodded and felt her bottom lip pull away from her gums. Her face went slack, growing numb, until she felt a quick stab followed by the soft slide through. Hannah thought there'd be more to it. But there wasn't much pain, and it seemed over before it began. In fact, the entire procedure was oddly soothing, as if she were being sewn together with gentle tugs of a thread. Then she sensed a ring clipped into place, the clasp like an invisible bite on her mouth.

"All done," he said. "Want to look?"

Hannah shook her head, refused to open her eyes. A bead of sweat ran down the bridge of her nose. There was nothing to do but sit and wait. It wouldn't be long before her body felt the strength to walk again. But until then she wouldn't move, wouldn't even speak, wanting only to run a tongue along her lip, inspect the fresh split of skin, at last allowing metal to touch metal.

LEFT BEHIND

Jill's father came over when the April air started to heat up, the temperature reaching well into the sixties. Carl watched Roy drive onto their gravel road, his white pickup rusted in the wheel wells. The bed was full of sandbags: fifty pounds apiece and stacked four high.

Carl stopped his father-in-law in the yard. "What are you doing here?"

Jill stayed inside to secure the house, peeking between the curtains.

"Things aren't looking good upriver." Roy adjusted his cap: its bill creased into a floppy V. He pounded a sandbag with his fist. "Start at the foundation. It'll protect for a little while."

This was the old man's first visit to the house since Carl and Jill had moved in last summer. Roy hadn't been invited today, either. He'd simply shown up after the phone lines went dead and he couldn't keep calling in the advice. "I told you we don't need your help, Roy."

"You can lend a hand or leave it be." He hoisted a bag on his shoulder and dropped it against the brick base of the house, went back for another. "That's up to you."

This wasn't Carl's first flood, but the water had never risen this high, this fast. It was no longer the Chickasaw River he'd come to know. Instead, it was just some melting surge flowing downstream. And this new water swelled everything, even the oxygen in the air. Carl sat on his porch, watched Roy go to work, and thought it strange how other people's problems always become your own, no matter what you do. And it wasn't supposed to crest for another two days.

When the last bag was put into place, Roy hollered, "I'll have to go back, get more."

"Don't do this to yourself." Carl followed him to his truck. "We can handle it."

Roy fiddled with his greasy cap. "I'd start getting things out you want to keep."

He didn't ask about Jill—didn't even ask to be let in the house.

"Go home," Carl said. "You're making it worse for yourself."

He got into the cab, fired up the engine until it roared.

"I mean it, Roy."

"I know you do, son. I just wish she'd come out and tell me herself."

As Carl watched the truck grind up the hill and disappear into the timber, he knew that if Roy's wish actually came true, it'd be the last thing the old man would ever truly want.

Carl sat and watched the stream, still several feet away from shore but no longer whispering by the embankment. No bubbling trickle over the rocks and stones. No riffle where fish fanned against the current. Things were expanding too quickly for anything to be seen through this kind of water, though strangely enough the river had been the very reason he chose this house.

Carl remembered Jill saying how, even after thirty-five years, she still loved the sound of its waters, the rhythmic murmur like an absent mother's heartbeat. So, after the wedding last August, he surprised her with a new home, driving straight from the courthouse just so he could carry her over their very own threshold. It'd been a small ceremony—no family, no friends, nobody to tell them no—but it felt like something bigger had brought them here, as if fate was finally making up for lost time. In fact, Carl liked that Jill was a bit older than him but still looked like she did all those years ago, when they were just a couple of kids stuck in the same bad situation—a place where when someone left they were usually gone for good.

But then, last spring, while fishing the Chickasaw—a small tributary of the Mississippi where he'd recently made camp—Carl went into town for a bite and saw the girl he once knew waiting tables. For years, he'd kept life simple: moving from one town to the next, following the day labor and living out of his truck—anything to avoid getting trapped in one place. But when he saw Jill and recognized that same sad look, the way she wore her loneliness like a uniform, it was as if life had bent back on itself, trying to tell him something. Like maybe she needed him. Or perhaps the other way around. Either case, it was as if he'd stumbled upon a crossroads that'd always been calling his name. So he hung around for a day, then two, until an entire week went by before getting the nerve to say hello. And though, at first, she looked confused, maybe even a bit embarrassed, she agreed to a drink. And then, that night, Jill never stopped holding his hand. So, it was only a few hours later, lying under the covers in a cheap motel, watching the girl he met years ago sleep the softest of sleeps, that Carl knew he was done with leaving things behind.

The river had risen by the next morning. Their basement windows seeped water, thick and red like blood. They had two boats, both tied to the dock and struggling in the tide. Carl measured how far it'd climbed overnight. It was close, creeping up the stilts that held the porch. Maybe a few more hours. Maybe not. They'd been through it before when a sudden winter warm-up had forced the Chickasaw to spread. But it'd crested quickly, leaving a wake of trash and rotten fish. The smell of death had been everywhere, like the river decayed as it shrank back into its channel. Except, now it was spring. This sort of thing always happened again. It should've been expected.

When Carl stepped into the house, Jill was crouched behind the refrigerator, unplugging it from the wall. He walked over and tipped it for her. "What else is there to do?"

"Not much we *can* do." Jill wiped her hands on her dirty jeans.

They hadn't slept yet: packing and making lists, crossing things off and making more lists. They grabbed food and appliances, spending most of the night on their hands and knees as they searched for things to save. The water rumbled in the dark, but they could never pinpoint where it was exactly, how far off. Even with the porch lights they couldn't find the water. It felt like it was already at their feet, though the echo of the current seemed miles away.

Now their bones ached, their skin grimy. Jill said all she wanted was to soak in a tub. "Lie in some clean water for once." Then she asked, "What do you think happened to him?"

Carl had been avoiding the subject all night. It wasn't like Roy to leave them alone.

"He's done this a hundred times," he said. Though outside, the river was twice as wide, a lake stretched across their backyard. "He knows what to do."

"Do you think he's okay?"

This new worry made Carl's mind go muddy. Far as he was concerned, Roy could reach out to them if he needed something. Always had before. "Let's think about ourselves."

Jill made her way out onto the porch. "He's probably already gone anyway."

"Probably." Carl followed, talking to her back. "Bet he's already in town by now."

She acted like she hadn't heard him even though he was right beside her.

"I don't think there's any chance this time," he said. "Let's get ready. Okay?"

But she didn't move.

They both just stood on the porch and watched the water rise some more.

Last spring, after that first night together, they never spent another one apart. Carl took a room at an extended-stay hotel, and each evening they'd watch a movie or take a walk, only to eventually make their way back to his bed. Jill didn't say much, and he liked this about her—her stillness. Plus, she let Carl be Carl. Never scolded him for being late or living paycheck to paycheck, going job to job. She claimed to actually admire his messiness. "Reminds me of what it'd be like to be young for once," she said, though he was only a couple years less than her.

One night, as they lay awake, staring into the dark and listening to each other breathe, their bodies still slick with sweat, Jill asked if he remembered anything about the group home.

"Just that I hated it there. Felt like the world had walked out on me. And then I met you."

When Jill got out of bed, Carl wondered if he'd said the wrong thing. Until she went to her purse and pulled out a small bundle. "Thought you might want this back."

Carl unrolled the cloth to reveal a black pocketknife inside. "I can't believe you kept it."

"May sound weird, but it helped more than you can imagine. Just knowing it was there."

"It was my dad's." He felt its heft through the fabric, but couldn't bring himself to grip it. "He got it in the Army."

"Didn't realize it was a family heirloom. Well, then I guess it's back where it belongs."

"Did more good for you than it ever did me." He rolled up the knife and handed it back. "Plus, you're my family now."

Jill squinted and smiled. "What are you talking about?"

When he mentioned marriage, making this thing between them lawful, Jill simply laid her head on his chest and said he didn't need to ask permission. She was happy either way.

"What about *your* daddy?" Carl asked. "Do I need to ask *his* permission?"

Jill said she was none of her father's business anymore, even if they did still live under the same roof. But Carl knew better. So the next day, while Jill was at work, he boated upstream to their house where Roy met him on the dock. Then, after tying up, the old man took him inside and said, "If your intentions are upright, I'll let you marry. God knows she deserves it."

Carl teetered on the edge of a rocking chair while Roy poured coffee into white mugs.

"After Jill's mom died, that girl was the only thing I had. Still is, I suppose. Though I'm sure you've heard all about that by now."

Carl shook his head and pictured his own ex-wife, living alone with their son—probably clinging to the kid like a life raft. For years, he'd tried to outrun these thoughts, but sometimes when he wasn't paying attention, a stray notion still slipped by. A look in the mirror and he'd wonder if his boy had the same cleft chin, those same angry eyes. On sleepless nights, when old memories took hold, he'd get curious if his son ever kicked the hornet nest of the past as well. And if so, was there hate in it? On good days, he figured hate helped more than most kinds of love. But at night it was tough to make this true. Carl knew all about the pitfalls a father could leave behind. He'd already lived too long in that same shadow to expect anything otherwise.

When Roy cleared his throat, Carl took a sip of coffee. "Jill doesn't talk about family."

"I bet she doesn't." The old man sighed. "Don't worry. You'll hear things. But all of that's just history now. You understand me?"

Carl nodded. "I know something about that myself."

"No, you don't. But you will." Roy grinned, rubbing his knees. "Don't tell her I told you this. Don't know why I'm telling *you* exactly. Except maybe it'll make a difference. Someday."

That night, as Carl proposed, he silently swore to himself it wouldn't turn out like before.

And even if Jill suggested they go someplace where nobody knew them, Carl was sick and tired of moving. It felt nice to be somewhere with a little history for once.

So after the wedding, as he pulled up to the *SOLD* sign, Carl made her a promise to never leave. "Because, Jill, finding you, right here, is the only thing that's made sense in a long time."

And when tears ran down his new wife's face, Carl assumed it was his words causing her to cry, especially when Jill leaned over, kissed him, and said, "Call me Mrs. Dunbar."

As the river climbed, they moved as slowly as possible. The need to leave the house didn't equal their desire to stay. Carl's arms ached from all the lifting. Pots and pans seemed made of concrete. Their clothes felt soaked with the air. The rickety furniture was like dragging bank safes across the floor. They decided to sacrifice these items to the flood. There was no time, nor energy, to waste on anything but necessities.

But as water finally crept into the house, Carl took his wife's hand and said, "Let's go."

"Not yet." Jill put down a box and led him to the back door to watch the river seep over the porch's edge. It was getting late. Carl had no idea how long they stood there, hypnotized by the current. He couldn't believe they were just going to hand over their place without a fight. That they were being betrayed by the very home they'd grown to love so much.

Jill slipped her arms around him.

"Don't worry," he said. "It'll all be here when we get back."

The trees, the shore—everything beneath so much water, he refused to look anymore. But before Carl could turn away, there was no denying the sight of Roy's boat drifting downstream.

Jill straightened up, sucked in her breath. "What do you think happened?"

The outboard twisted sideways, as if about to capsize right in front of them.

It was clearly deserted, which was comforting at first, though Carl felt the eerie impression of a boat without a captain and knew there was trouble in it.

"Do you think something's wrong?" she asked. Carl tried to pull Jill inside, but the river lured her back. "What if he didn't make it out of the house?"

Jill let him tow her to the front door where, outside, the morning was calm. Birds flitted between trees. The sun peeked out of the clouds. Everything was quiet, like any other day, except for the water that'd already washed out the road. Their pickup was submerged to its bumper. Carl waded out, opening the door against the stream. But as he turned the ignition, it only clicked.

"Jill, let's get the boat ready."

She stood on the stairs, squinting upstream and hugging herself as if cold.

Carl waded to their old motorboat, its towline taut with the current. "Jill?"

"I think he's in trouble."

"Roy has good instincts, honey. He knows what's best for him."

Jill wiped at her eyes. "No. He'd have come here. Something's wrong. I know it."

Carl looked over to their full truck bed, all the things they still had yet to salvage.

"He's an old man," she said. "We have to go check on him."

He gently took her shoulders, gave a little shake. "*We* have to leave now, baby. Listen, I'm sure he's safe somewhere. He's in less danger than us if we don't get this boat loaded."

Jill waved a hand at the house and said to let it float away. "I don't care about this stuff."

"You don't mean that."

"He's in some sort of rough shape." She was crying now, her chest heaving. "I know it."

"I can't believe this. You want to risk it all? For him?"

Jill cut him such a look that Carl knew he'd stepped into something bad.

"He's still my daddy. What if it was yours?"

"I wouldn't care if it meant losing you. Look!" Carl pointed to their tiny rowboat as it began to float into the house through the back door. "It's too late. We have to go."

"Fine. You leave. I'm going to see what happened."

She walked to their motorboat with a determination Carl had never seen. For all the phone calls, all the visits he'd had to intercept, his wife now wanted to make nice in the middle of a flood. What was he doing in this new family that was so full of the same old quarrels?

But this was a battle Carl knew he wouldn't win. And though it was a bad idea, he also knew that this wasn't her fight anymore. "Okay, Jill. Okay. I'll do it."

"No, don't worry," she said, getting in the motorboat. "You just save yourself."

He told her to use the rowboat, float toward town. "I'll go get him. If it's what you want."

"If you don't, I will."

She was about to shove off when Carl grabbed her arm so hard he felt it might fracture.

"Stop it now," he said, "I'll go."

She stared him straight in the eye, as if to make him understand. "Promise me."

And Carl did.

When they moved in, only Carl answered the phone. Jill told
him to always say she was busy, but Roy kept calling, asking
if he could visit a spell, talk to his daughter just once. At first,
Carl wasn't sure what was behind it. Inheritance issues? Blame
about a mother's death? Either way, he kept hanging up on
the new father-in-law, even when Roy said how proud he was
of his baby.

There was no easy way to their home, the river a faster
ride than the gravel roads, so it soon became a world divided.
Each night, when they stepped into the house—grease stains
on her apron, tool belt over his shoulder—everything seemed
so easy, so straightforward, something they hadn't counted
on becoming. Carl walked to the riverbed with a pole while Jill
fired up a grease pan. They ate off tin plates, the food fresh and
clean and not even tasting like fish. Then after dark, on the
back porch, they shared smokes, passed a can of beer between
them, and listened to cicadas hum in the trees. Leaf-canopy
hid the bright glitter of stars, the silver phases of the moon.
They didn't light lanterns, candles, fire. The only glow came
from the orange ends of cigarettes, which briefly brightened
their faces, suggesting more silhouette than shape.

They didn't always speak. But when they did, it was often
to fill in the last twenty years.

Carl and his small stint in jail; assuring her it was just
another dumb mistake. That the real justice arrived with the
divorce papers, asking for full custody. He fought it, but couldn't
do much behind bars. So, upon his release, Carl was ready to
make amends. Changed man and all. But when he got home
and found the place empty from top to bottom, he knew
change was just another word for walking away. So, he got

drunk and spent the night punching a hole through each wall he could find, figuring it best for everyone if he'd just call it quits. Even had a bullet in the chamber, as if the only path to setting things right was to get out of the way for good.

"What made you change your mind?" Jill asked, taking a deep drag.

"I don't know. Maybe I just didn't want people to say what I knew they would."

"What would they say?"

"How I was like my dad. Everyone always worried something had been passed down."

"What kind of something?"

"Don't know for sure." Carl dropped his cigarette, watched the sparks bloom at his feet. "Offed himself before I got a chance to ask."

Jill nodded. "Some fathers just aren't up for the job."

Carl let the words sink in, unsure of what to say. He was curious if there was some truth to this. If that's why he signed those divorce papers, sold the house, and never looked back. Or if maybe that kind of thinking just made things worse, people giving up on folks too fast.

"I'm not like that anymore," he said.

Jill told him to shush. "Those things don't matter. Not here. Not with me."

When Jill spoke, it was often about the funeral. How afterward, the image of her mom's waxy face brought nightmares. And how Roy was left with nobody in his life except Jill: old enough to cook and clean and looking a little more like her mom each day. Until one night on the porch, a bit tipsy and unable to say more, Jill took Carl's hand and traced his fingers along the raised ridges of her thigh. She'd taken his hand the same way two decades ago. And though back then she never gave an explanation, it almost felt close to a confession. But now, on the porch, allowing him to touch her scars again, Jill finally said the words aloud. How for years she was forced to be a woman before she knew what it meant. Her body becoming a kind of canvas for someone else's sorrow, so that she didn't know where else to put the pain except in her own skin.

Carl knew she had nightmares but didn't know they were full of heavy hands holding her down. And though a sudden burn rose in his chest, he had a hard time seeing the old man who offered him coffee as the same person who left behind all this hurt. "Why didn't you leave?"

"There was nowhere else to go. And, eventually, it ended. Just as fast as it began."

"Well, that's all over now."

"Some folks can forgive. Some even learn to forget. But I'm not one of those people." Jill stroked the welts on her leg, as if she'd carved them there for this exact reason. "Not anymore."

That night, they went to bed and made love as long as possible. Except Jill stopped with the hand-holding. She no longer wanted it slow or soft. Sometimes Carl held her so tight it felt as if her ribs were about to give. But whenever he relaxed his grip, Jill pressed against him, asking to not be let go. And over the year—after admitting that even if her father's desire went away, the threat of it still loomed in that home like a smell you couldn't get rid of—their own intimacy became more insistent, nearly drastic, as if trying to force the memory out of their bodies.

Then, in the morning, they'd skip breakfast, sip some coffee, and quietly go their separate ways. Carl tried not to think about it during the day. Instead, he focused on the present—a pile of sheetrock, the heft of a hammer—leaving the past for the dark when they were at last allowed to be themselves: natives in the woods, safe in the shelter of trees, a river surrounding their home.

With the water still on the rise, Carl went to retrieve their rowboat. He filled it with what he could and told Jill to get in, to stay along the edge. He'd be right behind soon enough.

She kissed him and said not to worry. "I've done this before."

But as he handed her a paddle, Jill grabbed hold of his wrist and said, "For protection."

When she placed the pocketknife in his hand, Carl wanted to drop it into the water, watch it float away forever. But Jill wrapped his fingers around the grip as if returning some long-forgotten favor. "I don't know. Maybe I should go with you."

Before she had a chance to change her mind, Carl gave the boat a shove into the current.

From the shore, he saw tears hanging from her eyes as she drifted downstream.

Their porch was submerged, water already in the house. He wondered how much was still worth saving. If insurance was enough to bring it back. Then he carefully slipped the knife into his pocket and yanked the ripcord, steering against the tide.

Because Roy's house was only a few miles upriver, Carl told himself there was nothing to worry about. But the angry way he opened up the throttle told a different story. So he took a deep breath and massaged the crick in his neck, knowing this was something rage would only make more difficult. He tried to think of that "other Roy." The man who gave him coffee and advice as opposed to the one who called all the time begging his son-in-law for something he just couldn't give. Carl still had never been able to merge these two versions of Roy, and maybe there was something to that—something there to rely on. Hell, maybe there'd even be some kind of hope at the end of this that'd make it all worthwhile. But when the terrible images of Roy returned—the old man sunk somewhere in his own house—hope seemed like an empty promise.

Instead, Carl focused on his own promises, grateful his wife hadn't come along. What would she have done, seeing her father like that: in trouble, if not already dead? Would she cry? Blame Carl for not moving fast enough? Or would she have no idea of how to act? Just like Carl, who had no clue what he'd find, or what he'd do when he found it.

It was twilight before he rounded the final bend and saw the house still standing. It looked abandoned, but Carl sensed something still alive about the place, something that couldn't be killed simply by water. He lightened up on the throttle and, realizing the dock had gone under, drove up to the building itself. The downstairs was still negotiable, so he moored the boat to a broken transom and crawled through. Once inside, the river reached to his knees.

"Roy! You here?" The house settled with a groan. Carl felt the joists shifting and tried to keep calm as he waded into the kitchen. A loaf of bread floated around his shins, and Carl knew he'd been right all along—Roy had already left. Until, of course, he splashed into the living room and saw the bulky shadow quivering in the corner, blank eyes staring out a window.

"Roy?" The word felt strange echoing over the water. "What are you doing?"

The old man, wrapped in a bathrobe, looked unaware that half his body was immersed.

"Roy," Carl said, working his way across the room. "It's time."

"I didn't think *anyone* would come." He didn't move, as if talking to himself. His hair lay smeared to his scalp. "Jill with you?"

"She sent me." Carl put a hand on the man's shoulder. "She's worried about you."

"More worry." Roy kept his gaze out the window. "That's the last thing people want."

"Do you hear what I'm telling you? We're in danger here."

"Son, I'm finished with it. You can tell her that if you want."

"Aren't you listening? She wanted to come herself."

Roy attempted a laugh, which was almost enough to give Carl a good reason to leave.

But then there were the man's eyes: lifeless and shiny, as if about to leak. He'd never noticed how much his wife had inherited that same look.

"I came when we saw your boat. Your boat's gone, Roy."

"I know." The old man gave a small grin, the thick whiskers like iron filings around his face. "I saw it float away. It really put up a fight, though. Held real strong to that dock. And when it couldn't hold on any longer, it just..." He made a motion with his hands as if to show the boat releasing from his grip. "Drifted away. It was something to see."

Carl slowly backed away, just a few steps, but enough to keep his distance. "Well, it terrified your daughter. Had to practically beg her to boat into town when all she wanted—"

"What did I tell you?" Roy said, raising his voice. "Don't lie to me, boy."

The anger seemed like a good sign. There was still fire there. But it also made Carl cautious: a fire that could burn in water was capable of anything.

He touched the outline of the knife in his pocket, just in case, and said, "She's out there right now, Roy. On her own. All because I promised to come for you."

Roy gave Carl a small smile. "You've done good. But it's too late. I just can't anymore."

"I'm not leaving without you." Carl felt the water rising up his thigh. "Jill's expecting both of us and I don't want to disappoint her. Do you?"

Roy opened his hazy eyes and shook his head.

"Now, I'm going to pull up right next to this window. You get ready." The house gave another shudder, and Carl knew it wouldn't be long now. But as he headed to the boat, wondering how to get the old man out of here, a gravelly voice called from behind: "Son?"

He didn't turn around. "Yes?"

"Are you sure? I mean, did she really say that?"

"Say what?"

"Did she really want to come back here?"

They started to power their way into town but eventually had to ease up when night arrived, the dark making it too dangerous to navigate at high speeds. So Roy cut the engine and steered from the stern. Carl turned on the bow's halogen lamp to search for any hidden debris, but it didn't help. There was nothing to look at, only water spreading out over land. Since the banks had run over, there was no longer any solid ground to guide them.

"You have an idea where we are?" Carl asked. But all he could hear was breathing from the back of the boat. "Roy?"

"We're close."

"Close? Close to what?"

"To your house."

Carl squinted over the side. "How do you know?"

"Lived here over half a century." He let out a snort. "Me and this river are old friends."

"What kind of friend does this to people?"

"It's still our home."

Carl clenched his fists, thinking how Roy wanted to stick around after the rescue, just to witness the collapse of his own house, until Carl said there wasn't time for such nonsense.

"Think *our* place is still standing?"

"Probably all swallowed up by now. Something to get used to around here."

"Every one hundred years, maybe."

"No such thing as hundred-year floods. That's just a scam invented by insurance agents."

"Well, at least it'll be covered then."

Roy shifted his weight, giving the boat a slight sway. "Going to rebuild, huh?"

"We really loved it."

"Stay if you love it. But it's still a lot of work. Never enough insurance for that."

Carl wanted to say it was enough for them. That starting over was sometimes the only way to fix things. Destroy the old world in order to build it anew.

But it was too late to get into this kind of talk. So mostly they didn't say anything at all, their mouths overwhelmed by the familiar smell that comes with still waters.

They were barely moving now, the boat simply bobbing up and down. Carl peered over the edge to see if they were caught in a current when he felt a dull jab in his side. No matter how he moved, the pocketknife dug into his hip with every rise and fall of the tide.

Carl unfolded the blade and dangled it overboard. Strange how he once craved the end of the day, hungered for this little brook that was now consuming his home. He tried to envision Jill's face upon arrival, a hero's welcome. But this was just another fantasy. Everything they'd built had, in fact, been destroyed in a single day. And he'd been unable to protect it, leaving his wife to drift downstream while he came back with what'd already been buried so long—making him wonder if, once again, he'd gone the wrong direction, chosen the wrong life to save.

When Carl let go of the knife, there was only a small plop followed by more quiet. He closed his eyes and listened to the waves lap at the boat with little wet slaps. That age-old ebb and flow of things. As if nothing ever crested, but just came and went as it pleased.

Until a sudden snap echoed along the bank. Carl strained his eyes and at last found land: the shady mound of timber, a dark trench of gravel road. But no signs of life.

Then it came again, like branches snapping from trees.

Carl spun the light. "Do you hear that?"

There was no answer.

"Roy?" Carl listened for another sound, anything to reveal that something had survived all this. He tried not to think about that worn-out porch finally splitting from the house, ripped down by all that weight. "Let's look around a little."

But the two of them just kept floating downriver with no indication of stopping.

Carl couldn't take any more silence. Even if it was just the sound of a sigh, there needed to be something said, some sort of response, some kind of reason why.

"Roy, you listening to me? Tell me you hear it."

Locusts chirped. The wind gusted. But beyond that, there was nothing left to hear except the soft hush of water washing everything away.

O.B.O.

The moon is still in the sky when she wakes in the back seat. With the apartment cleared out, empty of even a bed, her car was the only option left.

Yesterday, to celebrate her thirtieth, Hannah threw herself a reverse birthday party, sitting on the sidewalk with a sign that said *For Sale: $1.00—Or Best Offer*, practically giving everything away so that, within an hour, all she owned could fit in the trunk.

This morning, she crawls behind the wheel, puts the key in the ignition, and takes a deep breath—attempting to offer a little prayer, a blessing for the road ahead.

Except, she isn't quite sure what to say. So, instead, she shifts into gear and heads west.

Once outside Iowa City, she can only see four feet in front of her. A thick fog has rolled in overnight, the wet air turning cold for a moment, until the sun rises and burns the mist away.

Then it's nothing but fields, until she, at last, sees the turnoff for Highway 20.

***

In Dexton, the factory has gone silent, its smokestacks dormant for months—finally bled dry by what the state calls progress. All the land's been bought out, and the highway keeps siphoning money to Bridger, where today a young man makes breakfast for his seven-year-old son.

Carl's been awake all night, worried about the mortgage, the thirty-day notice, the fact that some fathers can't even keep a roof over a family's head. Ever since the layoffs, he's been completely housebound, a sudden stay-at-home dad, while his wife, Sadie, earns tips at the diner.

So, this morning, Carl sits in the kitchen and watches his son, Geoff, slurp cereal—then a whole day ahead with nothing to do but stare at cartoons and think about the future.

Of course, he's always been good under a hood, and his Grandma Greta knows the owner of a garage in Dexton who's willing to give Carl a chance, despite his recent legal troubles. Nevertheless, he can't help but search the Want Ads again, curious if he has any skills to sell besides being another number on an assembly line. At times, he considers enrolling at NCC, become something more than the other men in his family—except money is the main problem, so going into debt seems a bit like moving backwards.

Still, Carl's lived in Iowa his whole life, so today—like most days—he closes his eyes and imagines what's out there, waiting for him beyond the borders. All he does is dream about escape, from work and wives, even sons who'd be better off without another deadbeat dad.

Oddly enough, years from now, this part of his life will feel like a dream, some foreign world altogether. In fact, Carl will often have a hard time recognizing the person he once was: a man who abandoned his boy and never looked back—as if he'd been given a chance to do it differently and instead fell into that same old story. A decade will pass, and most days he'll find a way to live with himself. Other times, he'll still feel one sin beyond forgiveness—until one afternoon by the Chickasaw

River, while sanding a deck he rebuilt himself, a car will drive up the gravel road. The stranger will be tall and have long hair and say he's lost. Carl will see a shadow of himself in the boy's face. And though he's waited so long for this day to come, there's also no guarantee it'll turn out the way he wants. Only when Jill appears at the door, asking who it is, will Carl be able to find the nerve to speak, not just to introduce his new wife to his son, but also to reassure the boy that he's no longer lost, that he's in fact found the exact right place.

Along Highway 20, the crops roll by, corn stalks green in the August heat. Each field is perfectly square, the land as pretty as a postcard. Wind turbines rise along the skyline as Hannah passes one small town after another. Adair. Crayton. Greer. Each more remote than the next, places barely big enough to earn a mark on the map, until she sees the exit for Dexton.

Soon, Hannah pulls up to an open field, looks at the long grass swaying in the breeze. She's not sure what this place means, what happened in this pasture, but fifteen years ago, it'd been her mother's last request to be scattered here. So, today, she picks up a different urn and tosses its ashes to the wind, watches the dust settle to the ground. There was no will, so she can't be sure what her dad actually wanted, but Hannah hopes only to make her mom happy, reunited with her husband at last.

It feels like she should offer a few words, though once again, there's really nothing more to say. Instead, Hannah studies the meadow, drops the urn into the weeds, and drives down the road toward an old trailer that hasn't changed a bit, sitting there with the same rundown siding and fall-apart porch. At first, she wonders if this is a sign to stick around awhile, maybe revisit the past one last time—until she sees the telephone pole with a hoop still attached, leaning like a tree about to topple, as if to remind her that some signs don't always mean what they say.

***

A few miles away, on Main Street, only a few buildings remain open: a bar and an auto garage. A pawnshop full to the brim with other people's possessions. And, of course, a diner, where a cop sits with an old flame recently returned to town.

Heath had reached out first, inviting Gloria for a quick cup of coffee, not expecting it to turn into an afternoon of confessions. They haven't seen each other in thirty years, both of them middle-aged and married, though within the last year Gloria has lost both her husband and child, each in a different way. But it's not until the red-haired waitress fills up their third cup that Gloria begins to cry right there in the diner. Heath isn't sure what to do; is tempted to touch her hand. Instead, he admits he already knew about the funeral—had actually been there when her daughter was lowered into the ground.

Gloria wipes her eyes and says it's not true, that she didn't see him at the cemetery.

Heath confesses he stood out of sight, several plots away, not wanting to be detected.

When she creases her brow and asks why, he isn't sure if she means why he hid or why he went in the first place.

And he isn't really sure himself. Maybe it was to save her the trouble. Nobody wants an ex, much less the town sheriff, showing up out of nowhere, intruding on a poor mother's grief.

Or maybe he just wanted to save himself, unable to face what was right in front of him.

Either way, all Heath can think about now is his own daughter, how she's recently gone missing from his life, so that today the only thing he has left to offer Gloria is *I know what it's like to lose a child.*

He expects some questions, followed by a lecture on how his loss isn't the same as hers—which, of course, is true.

Instead, Gloria looks terrified when she asks, *How did you find out?*

Again, Heath's uncertain about what she's asking—how he discovered the news about *her* daughter? how he came upon the truth about *his* daughter?—but there's also something suspicious in Gloria's voice, a nervousness that reminds him of a moment from long ago when, once upon a time, he accused her of disloyalty, infidelity, about being *found out*. How, despite Gloria claiming she never cheated on him during his deployment, they called it quits anyway, his trust so broken it could never fully heal.

However, today, Heath isn't sure which line of questioning to pursue—always taught to let the criminal do their own confessing. So, as to not say the wrong thing again, he simply asks Gloria to tell him more about it, says he wants to hear it from her, which is when she offers her own secret—about the first transgression between them all those years ago, when she had no choice but to lose a child before it became a child, not wanting to be a teen mother raising a kid alone, while he was overseas—or even worse, never coming back, except maybe in a box—because she had dreams and goals too, though now these things feel pointless in the face of actually having a child, only to lose another one all over again, like some sort of punishment for the past—

And there she stops, breaking down once more.

Heath's not sure what to do with this new information. Part of him is confused, while another part is just angry—not so much at what she did or didn't do, but the fact that she kept it from him, which seems like the bigger betrayal, a sin that can't be forgiven—though years from now, after his own daughter has stopped talking to him entirely, only to move across the country with another woman, as if trying to get away from him for good, Heath will remember today and wonder if he's partly to blame. Curious what it is about him that makes every woman in his life hide, run away, always scared to share their secrets like he's the enemy instead of the one person they can trust to protect and serve.

But this afternoon, as Heath tries to add up the pieces, figure out the timeline, locate when things went so wrong, Gloria finally stops crying and offers an apology—for all of it. And when he asks if she has any regrets, Gloria nods and says, *Too many to count*, which makes him feel a bit better until she takes his hand and adds, *But not the one you'd expect*, which is all it takes to bring out the tears, both of them weeping for what they could've had but didn't keep.

The gas light turns on, and Hannah wants to risk it. But she also knows there could be another twenty miles between exits, forcing her to stop at the station down the street from her old trailer.

She tops off the tank and watches the bikers at the pump, two of them sneaking looks at her, followed by a few whispers and an occasional laugh: the sounds of men acting like boys.

Inside, she shivers against the sudden cold and takes in the familiar smell of Freon.

A girl sits behind the counter, no more than sixteen, but her belly already ripe.

Her nametag reads *Hello My Name is Betsy*, and she winces at the struggle to stand. In fact, over the fullness of her stomach, the cashier can barely reach the register to ring up the bill.

Hannah doesn't want to spend the last of her cash, a small nest egg that's sure to run out soon. So, she holds her breath, curious how good her credit is lately. While the machine crunches the numbers, Betsy says she's sorry for the wait. *There's not much reception out here.*

The attendant tries to make small talk—*where you from, where you headed*—but Hannah has no plans in front of her, and she certainly doesn't want to talk about where she's been, so a shrug will have to do, creating a miserable silence that makes them both nervous as they wait for a receipt, which eventually arrives, printed out and handed over like a ticket that's been punched, a final permission to depart—as if she's been offered some last-second pardon that almost allows Hannah to breathe again—until the girl asks if she's okay, is she lost, does she need a little help?

But before she can be given advice, or pointed in any kind of direction, Hannah shakes her head, signs her name, and walks out the door, the humidity hitting her like a heat wave.

Out the car window, massive sprinklers jut over rows of corn, irrigating the soil. It's the last month of summer and a drought has arrived. Of course, it's supposed to be a year of solid yields, but it's always difficult to depend on predictions. Some things simply refuse to take root, flying right past the sign that says *Now Leaving* despite being asked to *Please Come Back Again.*

ACKNOWLEDGMENTS

Thanks to the editors of the journals in which these stories first appeared, in an earlier or different form:

"Food. Gas. Vacancy." (*Shenandoah*, originally published as "Replacement Parts"), "Smoked" (*American Literary Review*, winner of ALR's Fiction Prize), "Birmingham House" (*Greensboro Review*), "Momentary Darkness" (*North American Review*), "Down the Line" (*The MacGuffin*), "Vanishing Points" (*Twelve Winters*), "Limited Jurisdiction" (*Chattahoochee Review*), "Replacement Parts" (*Saranac Review*, originally published as "Rochester"), "Anywhere But Iowa" (*North American Review*), "Separate, Bodies" (*Cream City Review*), "Left Behind" (*North American Review*, originally published as "Something They Hadn't Counted On")

Thanks to all my amazing teachers for their support and wisdom, including the faculty at Colorado State University—especially Judy Doenges and Steven Schwartz, who not only gave me insight into my own work but improved it beyond expectation. Also, thank you to the entire English Department at University of Northern Iowa for directing me down this path to begin with, particularly Vince Gotera—my first guide into the world of writing.

A very special thank you to Grant Tracey—teacher, mentor, editor, advocate, and most trusted advisor. No words can express how grateful I am for the years of encouragement, generosity, and inspiration. All roads lead back to you!

Thank you to Matt Alberhasky—my first and last reader—

who has spent more time helping my work than anyone. Thanks for the friendship and conversation, not to mention the most intelligent critiques a writer could ever ask for.

Thank you to my colleagues at Des Moines Area Community College—as well as all the brilliant visiting writers who've attended our *Celebration of the Literary Arts* festival, especially Bonnie Jo Campbell, Charles Baxter, and Caitlin Horrocks, whose words still influence my words.

Thank you to Benjamin Percy, the first to ask me, "When you going to get your book out? I think it's about time."—which served as a kind of permission I didn't even know I needed.

To the crew at Atmosphere Press for turning dreams into reality. Thank you to Megan Turner, for the astute edits, Alex Kale for her direction, and especially Kyle McCord, co-teacher and friend, who has taught me as much as he has his own students.

To my parents for all their years of support—as well as my brother, Scott, who lent all his books to me at an early age, opening that initial gateway into a life spent addicted to stories.

And last, but certainly not least, undying love and gratefulness to Laurie, Chloe, and Eli—the most permanent parts of me and the essential purpose behind my purpose.

ABOUT ATMOSPHERE PRESS

Founded in 2015, Atmosphere Press was built on the principles of Honesty, Transparency, Professionalism, Kindness, and Making Your Book Awesome. As an ethical and author-friendly hybrid press, we stay true to that founding mission today.

If you're a reader, enter our giveaway for a free book here:

SCAN TO ENTER
BOOK GIVEAWAY

If you're a writer, submit your manuscript for consideration here:

SCAN TO SUBMIT
MANUSCRIPT

And always feel free to visit Atmosphere Press and our authors online at atmospherepress.com. See you there soon!

ABOUT THE AUTHOR

MARC DICKINSON's stories have appeared in *Shenandoah, Cream City Review, North American Review, Greensboro Review, Chattahoochee Review, Beloit Fiction Journal, South Dakota Review, American Literary Review* (as winner of the *ALR* Fiction Prize), as well as other journals. He received an MFA from Colorado State University and now lives in Iowa with his wife and two children, where he teaches creative writing at Des Moines Area Community College.

Printed in the USA
CPSIA information can be obtained
at www.ICGtesting.com
LVHW040028220924
791599LV00005B/21